There was nothing here
in Bloomington, Indiana—
anybody who could got away!

For lack of anything better to do, the gang drove
through the University campus onto a street called
Fraternity Row. Even the buildings here seemed
snooty. And as for the girls lying all over the lawns,
they were the snootiest. There were guys
around too, washing their Mercedeses and Jags,
listening to rock on their transistors, flexing their
muscles for those girls.

"They sure look like they've got it made," Moocher
said, voicing what all the guys were thinking.
"That's because they're rich," Mike almost sighed.
"I wonder what it's like to kiss a coed," Cyril mused.

Suddenly Dave, who had been daydreaming as
they cruised along, looked up and saw The Girl.
She was tall, nearly as tall as he, and slim, but her
face was what held him. Wide, intelligent eyes, a
full mouth, a short straight nose, all framed by long
dark hair. She wasn't just a pretty girl. She was a
girl he'd give anything, anything to know . . .

Breaking Away

Special Edition

by Joseph Howard

based on the screenplay by

Steve Tesich

WARNER BOOKS

A Warner Communications Company

For V.N.G.
The Last Tycoon

Breaking
Away

1

The four of them always went swimming out at the quarry in the summer. They had been doing it for as long as they could remember, and here they were, out of high school now, still doing it.

They swaggered down a narrow dirt road that was almost completely covered over by thick vegetation, on their way to the water. The sun was shining brightly above, barely forcing its way through the foliage. Here and there, huge uncut blocks of stone had been set down on the road, blocking the path.

Mike, leading the way, was singing, and the others were humming along. The tune had started out as the Tex Ritter version of "Bury Me Not on the Lone Prairie," but it had strayed pretty far from its origins. Mike had made up his own words to the tune, and his three friends were hearing the premiere performance in the Western world of the new version:

"And when I die," Mike sang, considerably off key,

"Won't you bury me
On the parking lot of the A & P
Blow out the candles and blow out the
lamps
And light up my pyre with my trading
stamps
I had two books but I needed three
To deliver me from the A & P
I had three books but I needed four
To go to heaven and redeem my soul."

He finished with a flourish. Dave, the blond boy hanging back a little, said, *"Bravo, Mike! Bravo! Bellissimo!"* He carried a large bicycle trophy under his arm.

The others ignored him. Dave talked in Italian all the time now, ever since he had won an Italian racing bicycle in a distance race. Before that, racing had been his hobby, but now his world revolved around Italian bicycle racers, Italian food, Italian music. He was beginning to think he *was* Italian, and expected the other guys to go along.

The best thing to do was ignore him.

Cyril, long and skinny, and a foot taller than the others, looked down at Mike and said, deadpan, "Did you really make all that up?"

They kept on walking. As they got closer to the quarry, even larger blocks of stone began to appear, big enough to dwarf them. Some were so large they had to climb over them. It made them feel like kids again.

Mike was telling the others about his plan.

"I sent away for this stuff from Wyoming," he said. "It'll tell you everything. Since you don't believe me, maybe you'll believe it when you see it."

Mike thought they were all going to go away together and be cowboys or something.

Cyril wanted a few more details before he went away someplace to be a cowboy. "And we'd work on the same ranch," he asked, "and sleep in the bunkhouse together, eh?"

"That's the whole point," Moocher said. Moocher, who was as short as Cyril was tall, had a terrific build he worked on all the time. Short but strong, that was Moocher. And very loyal. But not the subtlest mind in the world.

He had a way of stating the obvious that ticked Cyril off. "I always miss the whole point," Cyril said, sarcastically.

Moocher tried to smooth things over. "It'd be nice to have a paying job again," he said, "that's for sure."

"*Niente lavorare,*" Dave said, "*niente mangiare.*"

That was the thing about Dave these days. It was bad enough he talked Italian, but every once in a while he'd say something you couldn't ignore, and then you had to ask him what he meant.

"What's that mean?" Mike asked grudgingly.

Dave was happy to explain. "You don't work," he translated, "you don't eat."

11

"That's a terrible thing to say," Cyril said. He thought Dave was carrying this Italian thing a little too far.

"Stop!" Cyril shouted, his voice bouncing off the quarry walls.

The others stopped in their tracks, and turned to look at him.

Cyril was standing stock-still, his hand over his heart, looking like a man in an advanced stage of cardiac arrest.

"It was somewhere along here," Cyril said dolefully, "that I lost all interest in life." He paused, turning to look for the exact spot where the tragedy had occurred. "Ah," he pointed, "right over there. I saw Dolores Reineke and fat Marvin." Cyril looked as if he was going to cry. "Why?" he cried out. "Why, Dolores?"

"They're married now," Moocher said. Moocher was very good at sliding a knife into a guy.

"You see what I saved you from, Cyril," Mike said, putting his arm around his friend. "Had I not told you about the two of them you never would have followed them out here."

Cyril considered this for a moment, and then slipped away from Mike's arm. "Thank you, Mike," he said solemnly. "You made me lose all interest in life and I'm grateful."

Having accomplished the destruction of Cyril's will to live, Mike saw the opportunity to cause a little more trouble. "My brother says he saw you and Nancy, Moocher," he said.

"When?" Moocher wanted to know.

Mike thought for a minute. "Last Friday?"

"Wasn't me," Moocher said. "I'm not seeing her any more."

They had reached the pool. They stood at the top of a cliff, one of three sheer rock faces surrounding a large, deep, dark pool of water below. Abandoned derricks jutted into the sky in the distance behind them, sharp reminders of when this used to be a working quarry. As they began the descent to the pool, Dave was humming softly. It was a Neapolitan song. Dave never hummed American songs any more.

As they made their way down the rock face, Cyril said, "I kind of miss school. You know, this will be the first time nobody's going to ask us to write a theme about how we spent our summer."

"Remember the Tomb of the Unknown Substitute Teacher," Mike said laughingly.

Moocher remembered. "She believed us, too," he said.

"When you're sixteen," Cyril said, "they call it sweet sixteen. When you're eighteen you get to vote. But what do you do when you're nineteen?"

"You leave home," Mike said. He took any opening that helped make his point about going out West.

Mike started skipping down the rocks toward the water, taking off his clothes as he went. As usual, the others followed his lead.

Cyril remembered something his father had said, about how it wasn't necessary to wander far and wide to achieve a worthwhile life. He offered this wisdom to the group:

"My dad says Jesus never went farther than fifty miles from his home."

Mike, Cyril, and Moocher swam in the quarry pool. Dave stood at the cliff's edge watching them, enjoying the beautiful day—part of the group, but separate from it, too. He held his trophy casually in one hand. It was a comforting presence to him. It helped tell him who he was— who he wanted to be.

He pulled the little Italian phrase book out of his pocket, and searched in it for the words that would express what he felt. After practicing once silently to himself to get the pronunciation right, he called down to his friends in the pool, *"Oggi fa bello, non è vero?"*

"Sure thing, partner," Mike yelled from the water. He was getting the handle on how to deal with Dave.

"C'mon in," Moocher shouted. Moocher didn't understand why a guy would come all the way out to the quarry and then not go in the pool. It didn't make sense.

Dave had an answer for that, too: "I read where this Italian coach said you should never swim after a race."

"Who's swimming" Cyril said. "I'm drowning."

Moocher and Mike splashed water on Cyril and then swam away to a safer part of the pool.

• • •

Later in the afternoon, the four of them were stretched out on the rocks, getting some sun. Mike was staring at an old icebox deep in the water, at the bottom of the quarry hole. He was far too relaxed to dive down and explore it himself. It was far more pleasant to just lie there and consider the possibility.

"Aren't you glad we got fired from the A & P?" he said to whoever might be listening. "Right now we'd be working."

"We didn't get fired," Moocher corrected him. "You got fired. We quit."

That was true enough, and Mike was indeed responsible for the fact that they were all out of work now and lying around the quarry taking the afternoon sun. Mike appreciated the fact that his buddies had quit in a show of solidarity, but if something good didn't come along soon, like going away to be cowboys, his buddies might start reminding him of why they were all broke. So he decided to put a good face on matters.

"One for all and all for one," he said.

Moocher, with his great grasp of the obvious, said what all of them had been thinking and didn't want to say: "There aren't many places, you know, that'll hire all four of us."

Good old Moocher. They all lay quietly for a while thinking this over.

Finally, Cyril broke the silence. "You know what I'd like to be?"

"Smart," Mike shot back.

Cyril ignored him. "A cartoon of some kind," he continued. A vision of Roadrunner filled his head. He saw lean black cats racing at top speed off precipices, only to stop, suspended in midair for a dreadful second, before they plummeted straight down to some awful, noisy fate.

"Man," he enthused, "that'd be great. Like when they get hit on their head with a frying pan and their head looks like a frying pan . . . with a handle and everything. And then they go b-r-r-r-r." He shook his head, from side to side, his lips slack and rubbery. "And then their head comes back to normal."

He savored the image for a moment. "That'd be great."

Mike stared at his friend for a long time. "How come you're so stupid, Cyril?" he asked finally.

Cyril seemed to give the matter a great deal of thought. "I don't know," he said. "I think I have a dumb heredity. What's your excuse, Mike?"

Mike leaned over and popped Cyril a good one on the arm, hard enough to make Cyril wince. Then Mike walked to the ledge.

After waiting until he was sure all three of his friends were watching, Mike dove into the quarry pool, deep and sharp and graceful.

The others talked among themselves as they followed Mike's progress toward the ice-box.

"You hear from your folks, Moocher?" Dave asked.

"Yeah," Moocher said, "my dad called. He says there's a lot more jobs in Chicago. He hasn't got anything yet."

Moocher's father was one of several men from town who had been forced to look for work elsewhere when the quarry began to be mined out.

In the dark water below, Mike had reached the icebox. They saw him open the door, go inside, and shut the door behind him.

"He wanted to know if the house was sold," Moocher said, one eye on the pool below. "They could use the money."

"You can come and live with me when it's sold," Dave said. "In Italy everybody lives together."

Moocher looked back down at the water. So did Cyril and Dave. Mike was still down there in the icebox, and they were starting to get worried about him.

Moocher decided to tell Dave what was on his mind. "Ever since you won that Italian bike," he said, "you've been acting weird. You really think you are Italian."

Every once in a while Cyril said something that was right on the button, and now he did it again. "I wouldn't mind thinking I was somebody myself," he said.

The three of them were now standing at the cliff's edge looking down at the icebox.

"Maybe the door is stuck," Moocher said.

Moocher dived in. Dave and Cyril followed an instant later. Moocher descended through the dark water until he reached the icebox. He struggled to force the door open, but was quickly out of breath, and shot up to the surface, the others following.

As soon as the three broke the surface, gasping for air, a loud mocking cry bounced off the rocks:

"Yoo-hooooo!"

They looked up toward the sound, and there was Mike standing on the rocks above them.

The three of them exchanged puzzled looks. It had to be some kind of trick, like when Houdini let himself be handcuffed and locked inside a safe and thrown into an icy river. But how had Mike done it?

Mike answered their unspoken question: "It's got no back on it!"

Laughing triumphantly, Mike prepared to dive again. He was getting into his most graceful position when something caught his eye. He stopped, and looked again. The group in the water, now swimming toward the rocks, had noticed something, too.

All the fun went out of Mike's face.

"What are they doing here?" he said.

High above Mike, on the other side of the quarry hole, stood three guys and three girls.

College kids.

The four friends hated the intruders without even knowing who they were. They were college kids, and that was enough. Their rich parents sent them to school to get rid of them, and they drove around town in their new cars and their new clothes, and they acted like they owned the place. Some of them even dated girls from the high school.

Mike's attention was caught by one particular guy, standing at the ledge a bit in front of the others. He seemed to be getting ready to dive. Mike guessed the guy had at least an eighty-foot dive down into the water, with rocks on all sides. Even a college kid wouldn't be stupid enough to try that.

But he did. The college kid pushed off gracefully, executing a beautiful somersault in midair, and descended in a perfect swan, slicing the water as cleanly as an axe.

Mike was stunned. College kid or not, the guy was obviously terrific. Even Mike couldn't deny it. What the college kid had done made his icebox trick look very small-time. Mike looked down at the other guys, who were standing on the rocks below. It was obvious that they thought the same thing.

"I've never seen anyone dive off from there," Cyril said.

Nobody else had, either. Ever. That was the whole point.

"Show-offs!" Mike said, as he started to climb down the rock toward his friends. He had lost all interest in doing his own dive. "They've got indoor pools and outdoor pools on the campus, but they got to come here."

Reaching the guys, he announced, "It's my quarry."

Cyril assumed a very dramatic posture, one he remembered from an old Mario Lanza movie he'd seen on television. "This hole! This quarry hole is mine!" he sang out.

Mike didn't need any trouble just then from guys who were supposed to be friends. "Hey, Cyril," he said. "Let's get out of here."

They picked up their clothes and headed out of the quarry, forming a straggly, defeated line, Mike in the lead, Moocher behind him,

19

then Cyril, who was keeping his distance from Mike, and finally Dave bringing up the rear, still holding his trophy.

"If they're going to come here," Mike said, "then we'll go on the campus."

2

The college kid's spectacular dive had spoiled the quarry for them, good and proper. None of them said anything, but it was entirely possible they would never go back.

That was just like the college kids. Who needed them, and the cars they drove in, and the rich parents who paid for the lousy cars?

The guys were in Mike's car now, which he was driving down the dirt road that led out of the quarry. He was driving a good deal faster than he should. An unlit cigarette hung from his mouth. He was mad, and the other guys were mad, and nobody said anything.

Dave's racing bike was strapped to the top of the car. It gleamed proudly in the sun, like a trophy.

Mike sped into Bloomington, past a huge billboard with the Marlboro Man on it.

Bloomington, Indiana, Mike thought. Anybody with any sense at all would get out of Bloomington, Indiana, and go out West to be a cowboy or something, and here were these rich kids being *sent* here. Maybe for punishment. The thing to do was be like that guy in the Marlboro billboard. He didn't look like he took anything from anybody.

They passed a car lot on the right. The sign said "CAMPUS CARS." Mr. Stohler owned it. Mr. Stohler was Dave's old man.

Moocher scanned the car lot. "Isn't your dad working today?" he asked Dave.

"No," Dave said, "the doctor told him to take it easy. He's taking Sundays off."

To Mr. Stohler, one day off a week was taking it easy.

They sped on by Campus Cars. As they passed City Hall, Cyril turned to Moocher. "That's where you go to get a marriage license, Mooch," he said.

Moocher, who thought a lot more about Nancy than he wanted to, said, "Yeah, so what?"

Cyril thought he'd scored a good one. He laughed out loud. The laugh changed to a howl of pain when Moocher hit him on the arm.

It wasn't until they'd driven all the way through town and saw the huge, starkly modern buildings looming in the distance in front of them that the guys realized that Mike was driving to the university.

If there was ever such a thing as snotty buildings, these were it. Snotty and arrogant. They seemed to glory in their contrast to the low, midwestern architecture of Bloomington. And Mike was heading toward them, picking up speed, obviously looking for trouble.

He turned onto a street called Fraternity Row. Enormous houses were set back from neat lawns, mixed in with newer low-lying buildings.

Most of the fraternities and sororities were situated along this street, except for the few that had been unable to find room there, and which, therefore, nobody wanted to belong to.

Mike slowed down. There were a lot of well-built guys hanging out on the lawn, showing off their muscles, passing the football around, washing their cars, listening to rock on their transistors. A few moles were even reading.

Moocher stared at the muscles. Mike stared at the expensive cars. He noticed several Mercedeses and Jags. It must be worth anything to some of those rich parents to get their kids out of the house, Mike thought.

Cyril stared at the sorority girls who were lying on blankets on the grass, sunbathing in bikinis. Cyril had never seen so many good-looking girls in his life. Having money must do something to a girl, he thought.

Cyril felt called upon to comment on this theory to his friends: "Going to college must do something to girls," he said. "Just look at them."

As they passed a couple of exceptionally fine specimens, Cyril leaned his head out of the car and shouted at them, "Hi, there. What's your major?"

The girls looked up languidly at Cyril, pinning him for exactly what he was—a cutter. They returned to their heavy-duty work on their tans.

"They sure look like they've got it made," Moocher said, still the voice of the collective unconscious.

"That's because they're rich," Mike sneered.

Throughout this exchange, Cyril had not taken his eyes off the girls on the lawn. "I wonder what it's like to kiss a coed," he mused. "I wonder about it a lot."

You're not the only one, the other guys thought to themselves. Except for Dave. Dave, as usual, was thinking about Italy.

But that was before he saw The Girl.

She was one of a group of two guys and two girls lazily throwing a Frisbee at each other. They were about half a block down from Mike's car. None of the guys was paying any special attention to them, what with all the other things to gaze at, until a poorly thrown Frisbee came across the street in a slow, wobbly lob and landed on the street in front of Mike's car.

Mike saw it and speeded up. The grounded Frisbee presented him with a golden opportunity. It was *their* Frisbee, and he would smash it under his wheels.

Just as Mike accelerated, the girl ran out into the street to retrieve the Frisbee. All Dave could see of her was the way she moved, kind

24

of sweet and awkward at the same time, and that was enough to break his heart.

Mike, advancing like a tank, reached the Frisbee first and ran over it.

Dave caught a glimpse of The Girl as she straightened up quickly as a deer would on hearing a hunter's foot snap a twig in the woods.

She was tall, nearly as tall as Dave, and slim and graceful, but it was the face that you noticed. Wide, intelligent eyes, a full mouth, a short, straight nose, all framed by long, dark hair. There was the sense of a quick, amused intelligence behind the face. She wasn't just a pretty girl.

You wanted to know her.

The two male Frisbee players ran out in the middle of the street and yelled at Mike. Mike saw them in his rear-view mirror.

This was going to be better than he'd thought.

"Hey," he told his buddies, "those guys are yelling at us." He slammed on the brakes.

It didn't require a Ph.D. to figure out what he was up to.

"Hey, c'mon, Mike," Moocher said, placatingly. "We're on their turf."

A little newsreel started to run in Moocher's head, foretelling exactly what would happen in the next few minutes. All Moocher and his buddies had to do was get out of the car, and all along Fraternity Row cars would stop being washed and footballs would stop being passed, and he and his pals would suddenly be surrounded by an angry sea of LaCoste shirts and

25

cashmere sweaters, and when it was over, they'd have to wash Moocher and the guys off the street with a hose.

No thanks.

The two male Frisbee players were still standing in the middle of the street, motioning for Mike to come back and fight. The two girls were trying to talk them out of it. Mike was gunning the engine.

And Dave was still staring at The Girl.

"They think they own the place," Mike groused.

"They do," Moocher told him.

Cyril decided to take a crack at avoiding the destruction of civilization as he knew it. "Besides," he said, "you've humiliated them enough. In ancient Japan when you ran over a samurai's Frisbee he had to commit suicide."

As Cyril started to laugh, Mike slammed the car into reverse.

The two male Frisbee players in the middle of the road started to come forward, thinking Mike was going to stop the car, and then get out and have it out with them.

Not what Mike had in mind at all. Continuing to gain speed in reverse, he roared right through the middle of the Frisbee players, scattering them like dry leaves, making them dive for cover.

Once again, Dave caught a fleeting glimpse of The Girl's face as Mike, laughing maniacally, made a U-turn and drove off in triumph.

The Girl stood in the middle of the road, her cracked Frisbee in her hand, staring after the departing car. A guy with a terrific build standing next to her, muscles bulging under his T-shirt, didn't look happy at all. He was memorizing faces.

"Dumb cutters," he said. "Townie retards."

Dave was riding his new bike happily through the streets of southern Italy. As he gazed upon the small houses with complete enchantment, a Neapolitan melody echoed in his head. He smiled at the happy people sitting on their porches. They seemed very happy to see him. He waved at them like a returning hero.

"*Buon giorno!*" he called out. "*Buon giorno!*"

He was not in the least distressed when none of the happy, smiling people answered back. Nothing could mar the pleasure of this lovely day.

He spotted some small children playing their happy games in the street and shouted out, "Hey, *bambino!*"

The children didn't answer him, either.

Because Dave was not in southern Italy but in good old Bloomington, Indiana.

Down the street ahead of him, a woman was shaking out a rug, the dust flying up and catching the sun, and Dave couldn't help but smile at her.

A big blond girl wearing a waitress's uniform came out of one of the houses and saw Dave. She called out to him:

"Dave . . . is Moocher home?"

Dave, lost in his dream of Italy, just rode by her. She didn't fit into his fantasy. In southern Italy, blond waitresses didn't come out of their houses asking about guys named Moocher.

An elderly Indiana couple who had known Dave's family all their lives watched Dave float by on his bike. The woman clucked her tongue sadly.

"He was as normal as pumpkin pie," she sighed, "and now look at him. His poor parents."

Mr. Stohler, a stolid, perpetually harassed man, sat at his kitchen table swatting flies. He did not look happy. He scanned the air for flies like an antiaircraft gunner checking the night sky for enemy planes. His ears pricked to the telltale buzz, then sighting his quarry, he swooped down on it, and smote the table a mighty blow. The fly flew away.

Mrs. Stohler, a woman who had retained some youthful style, was standing at the kitchen stove boiling water. She winced at the report of the flyswatter.

Mr. Stohler stared grimly at the table.

"It's that cologne he wears," he grumbled.

"Neapolitan Sunset, it's called," Mrs. Stohler said serenely.

Mr. Stohler mounted another surprise attack on a fly. He missed again. "Well," he said, "it smells like fruit punch to me, and it attracts flies."

If there was one thing Mr. Stohler was sure of, it was that he had enough trouble in his life, and now his son's insane fascination with Italy was responsible for flies in the kitchen.

Mrs. Stohler walked over to the kitchen table, coffeepot in hand, and poured some hot water into her husband's cup. She withdrew a packet of Sanka from her apron pocket, broke it open, and emptied it into the cup.

"There," she said with finality.

Mr. Stohler looked at the kitchen table. He didn't see anything on it but the cup of hot water with the Sanka dissolving in it.

"This is it!" he said.

"You have to watch your diet," Mrs. Stohler said.

"Diet," Mr. Stohler growled. He made the word sound obscene. "If anybody found out I was on a diet, they'd laugh me out of town. A diet."

"You know what the doctor said," Mrs. Stohler began. "At your age—"

"At my age!" Mr. Stohler spat the words out. "What do you mean, at my age?"

Mrs. Stohler knew that her husband was getting older—for that matter, so was she—and she also knew that he knew it just as well. "He says you have a bad heart," she said.

Mr. Stohler nodded. He couldn't argue with that. "Yeah," he said sadly, "but it's got nothing to do with my age." He sighed. "It's our son that's ruining my heart, Evelyn. What's he going to do? He wanted a year with those bums, so I gave him a year."

"It hasn't been a year yet," Mrs. Stohler said mechanically. She was used to defending her son against his father's continual disappointment.

"But, Evelyn," Mr. Stohler said. "Look what's happened to him. It was funny at first, but it's not funny any more. *Ciao*, Papa. *Ciao*, Mama. *Arrivederci!*"

"It's just hero worship," she sighed wearily. "He says the Italians are the best bike riders in the world and he—"

Mr. Stohler smashed the table with his flyswatter. "This is America, Evelyn. Only paper boys ride bikes—and they earn money doing it."

Mr. Stohler himself had had a paper route when he was a boy. And a bicycle. It was part of his image as a self-made man. Mrs. Stohler was well aware of this, and was afraid her husband was going to start telling her about the *Saturday Evening Post* route he had had when he was a boy. She wanted to avoid this if at all possible.

"He *did* win his bicycle," she said, "and he *was* quite sickly till he started racing and in three years—"

Mr. Stohler had heard all this before. He interrupted his wife. "So now his body's fine but his mind is gone. He used to be a smart kid. I thought he was going to go to college."

"I thought you didn't want him to go to college," Mrs. Stohler answered.

"Why should he go to college? I didn't go to college. When I was nineteen I was in the quarries ten hours a day."

"But most of the quarries have shut down," Mrs. Stohler said. She had heard all this before too.

"Let him find another job," Mr. Stohler said.

"But there aren't any jobs," Mrs. Stohler said. This was true, and they both knew it.

"Let him look, at least. Let him come home tired from looking. He's never tired."

"He's young," Mrs. Stohler pointed out.

Mr. Stohler knew that, too. "When I was young, I was tired," he said. "I had my own place at seventeen."

"He," Mrs. Stohler said, referring to her son, "says Italian families stay together."

That did it. This remark went to the heart of what had been bothering Mr. Stohler all this time. He slammed down his flyswatter and made his point with all the accumulated rage at his disposal: "BUT WE ARE NOT ITALIAN!"

"I know," Mrs. Stohler said, just as quietly as if her husband had not shouted. "It's just that I came from a big family myself . . . and it was really kind of nice. . . ." She smiled shyly, embarrassed at what she was about to say. "He thinks we should have another kid."

Mr. Stohler looked as if someone had just told him the Martians had parachuted into downtown Bloomington. "What!?"

Just then, the cause of his sorrow and distress came walking through the door wearing his sappy smile and carrying another trophy.

"Ah, *buon giorno*, Papa," Dave sang out.

"I'm your father, not papa," Mr. Stohler told his son.

"*Buon giorno*, Mama," Dave said.

"She's your mother," Mr. Stohler said. And then, although it pained him to do so, he couldn't resist commenting on the trophy.

"Whatcha do," Mr. Stohler asked, "win again?"

Dave had his hand in the refrigerator. He took out a wedge of Italian cheese and a hunk of Italian salami and began gulping them down with a pleasure compounded of several elements: he was hungry, the food was good, and the food was Italian.

Mr. Stohler stared ravenously at the food in his son's hands. Then he looked at the kitchen table, on which his wife had now placed half a grapefruit. Then he looked at his son again. He found it unbearable to watch Dave chew.

Dave, oblivious to the wild range of emotions coursing through his starving father's brain stopped eating long enough to answer his father's question.

With appropriate gestures, he said, "Yes, the victory . . . she was easy. But the promoter . . . *fondatore* . . . He says the Italian team . . . it will come maybe soon . . . and I will race with the best. . . ." He raised his arms and pronounced the beloved word: "*Italiano.*" And then, in amplification, he added, "Like the nightingale they sing, like the eagle they fly."

Mr. Stohler's gaze remained immovably fixed on the salami and cheese in his son's hand. He watched it go into his son's mouth. He could feel his own mouth water. He thought it entirely possible that he might die of starvation sometime within the next half-hour. He didn't think he would mind. But, before he went, he would make his point.

"Speaking of flies," Mr. Stohler said, "there's a lot of flies following you into the house."

"Fly in Italian," said Dave, "is *mosca.*"

"Well, in English," Mr. Stohler said, "it's a pest." He warmed to his topic. "And speaking of pests . . ."

Mrs. Stohler, from long practice, had no

trouble guessing what was coming. An argument. She tried to divert the conversation onto a more congenial path. "It's a nice trophy, isn't it, dear?" she asked her husband.

But Mr. Stohler wasn't going to be diverted that easily. Not while he was starving to death and his son was gorging himself on food and bringing flies into the house.

"Yeah," he said, "so what. I've lived fifty years without ever getting a trophy."

As soon as he said it, Mr. Stohler realized that perhaps his statement didn't make the point he had intended.

His son looked at him with compassionate eyes. "You never got a trophy, Papa?"

This was adding insult to injury.

"No," Mr. Stohler said, feeling the anger rise in his voice, "never, and what's more . . ."

"Here, Papa," Dave said. "I'll give you one. You are *Numero Uno*. King Papa."

Dave handed his father the trophy. Mr. Stohler was stunned. He was so stunned he didn't even think to refuse it. And before he could even think to give it back, his newly Italian son kissed him on both cheeks.

"Don't do that!" Mr. Stohler shouted, as mortified as he had ever been in his life. "How many times—"

Dave took the play away from his father again. "Now I have to go and take a shower," he said, seemingly oblivious to his father's anger.

Halfway across the kitchen, Dave stopped and looked around.

"Such a big house," he sighed, "and so few people. I wish I had plenty of *fratelli* and *sorelli* to greet me when I come and to wave when I go."

He walked out of the kitchen.

Mrs. Stohler sighed. She, too, would have liked a big family. Brothers and sisters for Dave, sons and daughters for her to feed and clothe and watch grow up.

Mr. Stohler looked down at the trophy in his hand, as if trying to figure out what it was.

Just then, the lilting, hated sounds of Neapolitan music came wafting into the kitchen from the phonograph in Dave's room.

It occurred to Mr. Stohler that in later years when people told the story of the monumental rampage he felt that he was about to embark upon, they would say that this was the moment his mind had snapped.

"There's that music again," he said grimly. "I'm going to have it out with him now."

He headed purposefully for his son's room. He still had the trophy with him. He carried it like a weapon.

Mrs. Stohler followed her husband for a few steps, and then stopped. She waited, apprehensively, listening. She heard nothing.

She wanted to help her son, but her shoes seemed nailed to the floor. She wrung her hands, wondering if it were possible for a man to crush a teen-age boy's skull with a bicycle trophy without making any noise.

At that moment, her husband reappeared, looking as if he were the one who had been hit over the head. The trophy itself dangled limply from one hand.

"What's the matter?" Mrs. Stohler asked. The only thing she could think of that would

34

make her husband look this way was if he had gone upstairs and found their son dead before he had had the chance to kill him.

"He's straightening his hair!" Mr. Stohler told her. He sank down in a chair.

3

Enrico Gimondi, that great Italian star, was singing on the phonograph in his lilting Neapolitan way. Dave hummed along as Enrico sang about the joys of being young and in love in the summer in Naples.

He had transformed his room into a little Italian enclave right in the middle of Indiana. Racing trophies were everywhere. A man would have to be at least a hundred years old to have won as many racing trophies as Dave had in his room.

Then there were the posters of Italian racers. And the posters of Italian movies. There was even—and Dave had been in ecstasy the day he had found it—a poster of an Italian movie starring Italian racers. There were Italian magazine covers and pictures clipped from Italian racing magazines.

Wheels, cranks, pedals, chains, gears, handlebars hung from the ceiling, making it almost impossible to enter the room without getting hit on the head. Several bicycle jerseys hung from the doorknob.

Having finished shaving, Dave came out of the shower humming, making his way through the metal maze.

The family cat yowled at him, announcing that it was time to eat.

"Ah, there you are, Fellini," Dave greeted the cat happily. "Hungry, eh?"

The cat, whose name, until recently, had been Jake, and who was still called Jake by everyone except Dave, seemed to respond to his new name. He was hungry and they could call him Frank or Ralph or Enrico Gimondi, as long as they fed him.

Dave went to a bureau drawer and took out a can of Chef Boy-ar-dee spaghetti and meatballs. Still humming along with Enrico, he dumped the contents of the can into Fellini's— formerly Jake's—new dish, which was a deep ashtray with the Cinzano logo printed on the sides. He set the dish down in front of the cat and sang, *"Mangiare . . . mangiare . . ."*

The cat did as he was told.

Dave gazed at the posters of the Italian bicycle racers. Then he looked in the mirror. Then he took out a comb and began to comb his hair. What he was doing soon became apparent. He was trying to *become* an Italian bicycle rider. He combed his hair back, straight and slick, in the Continental style. When he was done, he looked at the results in the mirror and smiled with approval.

He picked up his Italian phrase book and lay down on the bed with it, prepared to learn a few new phrases.

About a half-hour later, in another part of town, Dave's father was looking at himself in a mirror. He checked his cuffs, the press of his pants, the roll of his jacket lapels. What Mr. Stohler was trying to do was look honest and helpful.

It was time to start selling used cars again.

"Campus Cars" was called that for the same reason stores in New York nowhere near Fifth Avenue were called "Fifth Avenue Fashions." It sounded good, it sounded prestigious, it sounded like the market Mr. Stohler was trying to attract.

The market, of course, was students. Kids from out of town with money in their pockets. Kids who weren't in Bloomington very long before they found out that they had to have a car if they wanted to get anywhere in town. Mr. Stohler was there to fill that need.

The signs around the lot didn't even hint at this. Instead, they said things like "BEST DEAL IN TOWN" and "CARS WITH A COLLEGE EDUCATION."

Mr. Stohler's most creative efforts were expressed in the signs that adorned the cars themselves. He gave all the cars names. One was called "GRAD SCHOOL SPECIAL," another "ENGLISH MAJOR," another "Ph.D." There was "CUM LAUDE," and next to it, "MAGNA CUM LAUDE."

Mr. Stohler's first customer of the day was a young blond boy in a red cashmere sweater that looked like it was worth more than any car on the lot. Mr. Stohler was trying to sell him a little sports job, "HOMECOMING QUEEN." "HOMECOMING QUEEN" was perhaps the finest name Mr. Stohler had ever come up with. It suggested that if you bought this snappy little job, the Homecoming Queen herself would fall madly in love with you.

But Mr. Stohler wasn't talking about that to the kid in the red cashmere sweater. Instead, he was talking economy.

"It gets thirty miles to a gallon," he was saying. "Of course, the mileage you get may vary. It's a beaut, right?" He knew better than to wait for an answer; he answered the question himself. "Right. You sure know how to pick them."

Then, having implanted in the kid's mind the idea that he had already bought the car, Mr. Stohler went on to congratulate him on his wise choice. "Frankly, this is the best car on the lot," he said, reeking sincerity. "Quality product."

At this point, Mr. Stohler paused to wait for a reply—just like the salesmanship manuals said you should. This was to give the kid a chance to say something like, "Yeah, you're right, it sure is a quality product."

Which is what Mr. Stohler expected to hear.

Instead, a loud, cheery voice hollered out, "*Ciao*, Papa!"

It was Dave, of course, on his bike, hollering and waving from across the street.

Mr. Stohler pretended not to hear anything, but the kid in the red cashmere sweater had heard Dave holler out, and turned around to see who it was. Mr. Stohler gave an expressive shrug that said, "I don't know—you know how it is—there's all kinds of crazies around on the streets these days," and turned his back. He sneaked a quick look over his shoulder, hoping his son had disappeared.

Dave was riding away.

Dave kept on riding until he got to the university. He hadn't consciously headed in that direction, but now that he was on campus, he was happy.

He was an Italian tourist. He was Enrico Gimondi, seeing the sights.

He was more than a tourist. He was more serious than that. He was an exchange student. He was honored that his parents, who were simple peasant folk, had struggled so hard to send him here, to the University of Indiana at Bloomington, and he would work hard and make them proud of him, and make more of his life than his parents had done, so that, in their turn, his children would do the same.

He marveled at the limestone classroom buildings, rising like obelisks out of the earth. He had heard that the fathers of the native boys labored in the stone quarry near the town to build these magnificent structures. Most of the men could not afford to send their children to the university, but they built the structures just the same. The local men took pride in their work, as Enrico's own father did.

Enrico saw students sitting on the steps of

41

the buildings, or lounging on the grass, walking to and from classes, all of them with their books in their hands. They seemed to take the buildings for granted. They probably took the books for granted, too. They did not understand what a wonderful country America was, where they could lounge before buildings like these and carry books that contained all the knowledge of the world, and be instructed by wise men who had studied long and hard to master their subjects. Enrico understood. He knew what a rare privilege he had been given, and he would not take it lightly.

Dave parked his bike and sat on the grass with his Italian phrase book. If he could master this book, he would really be Enrico Gimondi. He would have a place in this world. Then, as Gimondi, he could go on to master everything else. But first, this book—the knowledge contained in it represented his ticket of admission to a world his father had never mastered and so pretended to have contempt for.

A campus police car drove by, and Dave hid his face in the phrase book. He knew the campus cop, and it wouldn't do to be discovered like this.

When the car had passed, and it was safe, he looked up from the book . . .

. . . and saw why he wanted to be Gimondi, why he wanted to be somebody other than Dave Stohler, son of a used car dealer from Bloomington who used to work out at the quarry.

The Girl came out of one of the classroom buildings, books and papers in her hands. The wind was blowing her dark hair around. She clutched the books and papers to her. She looked so lovely that Dave thought he was going to faint.

His jaw hung slack. He blinked. He swallowed.

"Mama mia!," Enrico Gimondi said aloud.

He watched her walk. She seemed to have a glow around her, separating her from the rest of the world. He was sure he had never seen anything more beautiful in his entire life.

As she walked along, she switched her books from one hand to another. A piece of paper got away from her and blew away in the wind.

Enrico Gimondi saw it.

He now had a mission in life.

Like a knight of old, he was prepared to risk life and limb to see that the beautiful princess got her piece of paper back.

As he got to his feet, he could see The Girl trying to recapture her paper. The traffic on the street was too heavy for her to risk chasing it. She gave up trying and turned away, the expression on her lovely face so forlorn that Enrico thought his heart, which had nearly burst a moment ago, would now break. As she walked to the parking lot, Enrico got on his bike, and rode off to rescue the escaping piece of paper.

He cut through traffic. He cut in front of cars. He caused several people to slam on their brakes. He caused the same people to slam their hands down on their horns. Enrico didn't hear any of it. He was a man with a mission. He did intricate slaloms, half figure eights, weaving through the pedestrians, as if he were in an obstacle race. He was brilliant. Nothing mattered but the paper.

43

As Enrico sped along after his quarry, a college guy came ambling along, a cardigan-sweater type with books under his arm, and the paper floated by him in the air. The college guy reached out and plucked it out of the air, a brilliant one-hand catch.

He was just about to read it, when Enrico, speeding by on his bike, made another brilliant one-hand maneuver, snatching the paper out of the college guy's hand, on his way down the road in search of the beautiful princess.

The college guy, staring after the bike, wondered what it was that made people so crazy these days.

The Girl was riding home on her motor scooter. She saw something in her rear-view mirror. It looked like a kid on a bike. He seemed to be gaining on her. Instinctively, she speeded up.

Behind her, Enrico, the paper in his mouth, shifted gears and speeded up himself, not wanting to lose her.

The Girl looked in the rear-view mirror again. She saw the kid on a bike, closer than before and gaining. He had a piece of paper in his mouth. It occurred to her that it might be her piece of paper. Smiling a little, she increased her speed.

Behind her, Enrico was close enough to shout out and be heard. When he opened his mouth to do so, the paper flew out, but he recovered it with another swift one-hand catch, and hollered, "*Signorina . . .*"

The maneuver cost him ground, but he

stuck the paper back in his mouth, and pumped extra hard, pouring on speed.

The Girl passed a light just as it went red. There was nothing for Enrico to do but run the light, which he did, nearly getting killed several times in the process. He followed her up Fraternity Row, catching up as she was turning into the driveway leading to her sorority house.

He shot ahead of her, on her right, as she was about to make a turn into her driveway, and she, like so many others that afternoon, had to slam on her brakes to avoid hitting him. Enrico slammed his, too. They both came to a dead stop.

"*Signorina*," Enrico Gimondi began. As he was about to hand her the paper, he noticed that it was wet, as a result of having been in his mouth. He retrieved the paper, wiping it off on his biking jersey, and handed it to her again.

"It is yours . . . no?"

The Girl took the paper and smiled. Enchantingly. Then she laughed, and the laugh, if possible, was even more enchanting than her smile. Full and bright and merry.

Enrico felt amply rewarded right then. He would have swum the Tiber with her entire armload of books and papers in his teeth, just to see her laugh and smile like that. But then he got the real whammy: he heard her voice.

"You mean you've been chasing me with this?" The Girl said. "Well, that's really something. Thank you very much. Talk about chivalry."

Dave had never heard a voice like that— soft and mellow, hinting of secret amusements, with a vague accent he couldn't quite place. He hadn't heard what she said exactly. He was just

45

listening to the sounds she made, and the music in them.

The Girl, for her part, looked puzzled. She was accustomed to having guys stare at her, but not in the way that this guy was staring at her. She didn't know what he wanted, what he was up to, and it confused her.

"Well, thanks again," she said.

"Is nothing . . . *niente* . . . *signorina*," Enrico Gimondi said, recovering his identity in mid-sentence.

The Girl thought she understood why this gallant young man was looking at her so strangely. He was a European. Europeans had a different attitude toward women. That explained a lot. She had wondered at first why someone would dare follow her, when everybody on campus knew she was going with Rod, who was about as big a BMOC as you could get, and a jock to boot, and who would certainly flatten anybody who tried to come on with her. But a European couldn't be expected to know that.

"What're you," she asked, "an exchange student or something?"

Enrico Gimondi's smile was radiant. He basked in her understanding. "*Sì*," he said. "I am *Italiano*. My name is Enrico Gimondi!"

Dave had never said that to anyone in the world, but he knew, as he said it, that he would try to be Enrico Gimondi for her.

"And mine is Katherine Maxwell," she said, extending her hand for a friendly handshake.

"Ah, Katherina!" Gimondi exclaimed, and bent over and kissed her hand.

She liked having her hand kissed. And she

46

liked the way her name sounded on Enrico's tongue. But the way he kept staring at her was unsettling, European or not. She wanted to see more of him, she thought, although she wasn't sure why.

"Well," she said, "thanks again, again."

And smiled that smile.

"*Ciao*, Katherina," Enrico Gimondi said, and got on his bike and rode away, taking with him a precious gift that she was hardly aware she had given him.

Her name.

Katherine Maxwell.

He knew her name, and where she lived. He could find her whenever he wanted to.

Enrico Gimondi was so cool, so European, that he didn't even turn around, and so missed seeing Katherine Maxwell watching him ride off, a puzzled expression on her lovely face.

4

Nancy decided it was time to go over and see Moocher.

Nancy was the big blond girl in the waitress uniform who had called out to Dave about Moocher the day Dave was riding down the street being Enrico Gimondi.

Nancy was the girl Moocher had told his pals he wasn't seeing any more.

Which was why she decided it was time to go over and see him. This business of not seeing each other had been going on for weeks now, and Nancy had made a Major Decision about her life, and there was no point in making a Major Decision, one that would affect Moocher, if Moocher didn't even know about it. So she cast foolish pride aside and made her way up the scrubby lawn, past the CAMPUS REALTY sign that said FOR SALE, and knocked on Moocher's door.

He appeared, holding at shoulder height a barbell half as long as he, looking very casual about it, as if he hefted big barbells around all the time.

They smiled nervously at each other. They were both embarrassed, because each had tried to be the one who didn't give in first, and now here they were, looking at each other, very glad to be in the same place, and neither wanting to be the first to say so.

"Nancy," Moocher said. It was an opening that didn't give away too much.

"I was just on my way to work," Nancy said.

Moocher knew it was a lie, but he was so happy to see her that he didn't want to call her on it. He was grateful for her presence, and magnanimous in his triumph. With one end of the barbell, he casually pushed the door open and said, "Come in."

As Nancy passed him, Moocher checked the street to make sure nobody was watching. People in Bloomington had nothing to do but talk.

Once she was inside, Moocher closed both doors to the house. The back door was only a fast twenty feet from the front of the little two-roomer, but it was Moocher's place now, the doors were closed, and people could say whatever they wanted.

Nancy was a little surprised at what she saw. She had expected Moocher, with his folks gone, to be living a Spartan existence, spending all his time working out in order to maintain his terrific build, but it was still something of a shock to see nothing on the floor but a sleeping bag and a wooden footlocker.

No chairs, no tables, no nothing.

An absolutely empty house, with only the footlocker and sleeping bag in it. And Moocher, of course, who was now lying on his back on the floor, raising and lowering the barbells, working on his terrific build.

But she had come this far, and she loved him, and she thought it very brave of this little guy to be into physical fitness the way he was. So she sat down on the footlocker and looked down into Moocher's straining face and tried to tell him what she had come to say.

"You know what?" Nancy said softly.

"No, what?" Moocher said, doing a clean press and jerk.

"I'm leaving home, that's what," Nancy said.

Moocher stopped his barbell action in mid-air and sat up. "What! Where're you going?"

Nancy had the impulse to really shake him up, but there was nothing in her but the truth.

"About five blocks south. I found a nice little house to rent. It's so cute I could scream. My folks said I could have some of their furniture from the basement."

And then, having told him the whole story, and knowing it was far less glamorous than either of them would have wanted it to be, she tried again to make him a part of things, to get him involved in her fabulous new life.

"Maybe you could give me a hand," she said, ". . . moving."

Moocher, seeing how things were, started pumping the barbells up and down again.

"Sure . . ." he said, in between pumps. "If . . . I'm not busy. You know. How's the job?"

And that's when Nancy betrayed herself, letting her real excitement slip over, because out tumbled the thing she had wanted to share with him all along, the thing she had really rung his doorbell to tell him. "You know what? Frank said if I keep up the good work it'll just be a matter of time before I become a head cashier."

Suddenly Nancy felt embarrassed and wanted to leave. She got up from the wooden box. "I should go now," she said awkwardly.

Moocher didn't want to let her go, but he wasn't going to lose his cool and come right out and say it. Instead, he said, "Maybe . . . eh . . . Maybe I'll walk you to work. I have to go that way anyway."

Nancy smiled and headed for the door.

Dave and Cyril were on the outskirts of the campus. Cyril, in sweat pants and a T-shirt, was jogging. Dave was on his bike, riding very slowly, keeping pace with Cyril. They passed the Campus Arts Cinema, named, like Mr. Stohler's used car lot, to attract the student trade.

Dave looked at the marquee. It announced: FELLINI'S AMARCORD. Not just AMARCORD, but FELLINI'S AMARCORD. Those Italians had style, Dave thought.

They came to a place where some kids were playing basketball, using a flat metal hoop nailed to a garage for a basket. Cyril couldn't help himself. He jumped into the game, stealing the ball from one of the kids, dribbling down the court, very flashy dribbles, fading away, looking back, finally shooting a long jump shot. Right in. Two points.

He walked back to rejoin Dave, but couldn't help looking back. He missed the game.

Later, when he was running hard, with Dave still riding along beside him, Cyril asked, "Are your parents asking you what you're going to do?"

"I think they're getting curious," Dave said.

"I sure miss playing basketball," Cyril said. "I got depressed when my athlete's foot went away."

He ran a few more yards in silence, and then he said, "I was sure I'd get a basketball scholarship. My dad was sure I wouldn't. And when I didn't he was real understanding." He shook his head at the memory. "He loves to do that. Be understanding when I fail."

Cyril produced a fair approximation of his father's voice: " 'That's all right, Cyril, I understand.' " He continued in his own voice: "He even bought me a guitar because he was sure I'd never learn to play it."

Dave didn't know what to say, so he didn't say anything. Instead, he turned the conversation back to where it had been a moment ago: "I'm supposed to take this college entrance exam."

Cyril seemed surprised. "You going to college?"

"No," Dave said. "I'm just curious to see if I can pass."

"Maybe I'll take it, too, and flunk it," Cyril said. "My dad's birthday is coming up."

They came to the place in the road where they had to go in different directions. Dave rode off, and for a long while, Cyril stood watching his friend fade into the distance.

Katherine was driving Rod's snazzy Mercedes convertible. It made her nervous. She kept looking from the road to the rear-view mirror, back and forth.

"Just keep it steady," Rod shouted at her.

Rod and five of his fraternity brothers were on bicycles behind her. Rod was coaching his brothers, trying to turn them into bike riders as good as he was, and Katherine was supposed to be the pace car. Rod thought it showed a great deal of class to have a Mercedes convertible driven by a pretty girl as the pace car.

"Keep your elbows bent," he shouted at his riders. "That's right!"

He looked ahead to see a nervous Kathy slowing down. One of the bike riders almost smashed into her. Rod didn't want that. He didn't want a busted-up bike rider, and he didn't want a paint scratch on his trunk, either.

"Pick it up, Kathy!" he shouted. "Thirty an hour!"

Kathy stepped on the gas.

Further on up the road, Dave was out riding his bike, lost in his fantasies of Italy. It was a glorious day, and he felt glorious.

Then his lovely mood was shattered by what sounded like a pistol shot. Only it wasn't a pistol shot, he learned as his bike began to wobble violently, it was the sound of a tire going flat.

"Ah! *Stroonz!*" he exclaimed, and put on the brakes.

54

Fortunately, the great Gimondi knew what to do in emergencies like this. The great Gimondi was a master of maintenance and repair. A few moments later, he was taking the front wheel off, peeling the tire off the rim, getting ready to put on the spare he kept for such situations.

A Mercedes convertible came down the road toward him. It was being driven by the beautiful Katherina.

Gimondi did not like the idea of the beautiful Katherina seeing him in such a humiliating position. . . .

On seeing Gimondi, Katherine had slowed down a little, just enough to cause Rod to almost bump into her.

"What are you doing, Kathy?" Rod shouted.

Rod was getting mad. If you asked a girl to drive the pace car, the least you could expect her to do was maintain a steady speed.

Kathy speeded up, and the bike riders swept past Dave. As he sat pumping up his spare, he could see the legend on the backs of their jerseys: LITTLE 500.

Gimondi looked after them with contempt. He had won far greater races in his day, and would again, just as soon as he got this tire back on.

Mr. Stohler was seated at the kitchen table. He was telling his wife how his day had gone, and adding a little personal philosophy.

"Those college kids aren't so smart," he was saying. "I sold one of my worst cars to one of them today. They're not so smart. It's a good thing that Dave didn't . . ."

55

He stopped cold in the middle of his sentence and took a closer look at what his wife had just placed in front of him.

"What's this?" he asked.

"It's sauteed zucchini."

That's what he had been afraid of. Now they were bringing zucchini into his house. Zucchini reminded him of Italy, which reminded him of Dave, which reminded him of Dave hollering "Ciao!" at him and almost messing up his sale to the kid in the red cashmere sweater. He didn't know what he was going to do about Dave.

"That's Italian food," he said. "I don't want it."

"No, it's not," Mrs. Stohler said. "I got it at the A & P. It's like squash."

It didn't look like squash to Mr. Stohler. "I know Italian food when I see it," he said. All that 'ini' stuff. Zucchini . . . fettucini. . . .I want some American food." Then he thought of his diet, and all his sorrow came tumbling out. "I want some french fries!"

The cat, smelling the zucchini and having no prejudice against Italian foods, jumped up on the table.

"Get off, Fellini," Mrs. Stohler said.

Mr. Stohler exploded. "THAT'S MY CAT!" he shouted. "AND HIS NAME'S JAKE, NOT FELLINI." Then, a bit more calmly, he said, "I won't have any 'ini' in this house."

Looking at the offending cat, he raised his voice again. "YOUR NAME IS JAKE. UNDERSTAND?"

The cat looked blankly at him.

• • •

Dave didn't get home till late that night. All the lights in the house were off. He had his bike with him, and he was trying to sneak up to his room without being heard.

Mr. and Mrs. Stohler lay in bed, staring at the ceiling. Neither of them spoke. They were thinking. Especially Mr. Stohler. He was thinking about zucchini and Italian names for cats.

Mr. Stohler heard a light sound on the stair. "He's back," Mr. Stohler said to the ceiling.

The next morning, Enrico Gimondi was outside in the sunshine, oiling his bike. It was this kind of careful maintenance, painstaking and craftsmanlike, that made Gimondi the champion he was. An unoiled bike was unthinkable to Gimondi. Even if he did not intend to ride it that day—a rare occurrence in itself—he kept it oiled. If he did not, he would feel the difference in his blood.

The mailman came walking down the street, handed Gimondi the mail, and went on his way, neighborhood dogs barking at his heels.

Gimondi looked through the bills and leaflets and found his copy of *Sports Illustrated*. Leafing through it on his way to the house to bring his mother the mail, he noticed an article that made him drop everything else in his hand and head for the house on a dead run.

His mother was coming out of the house as Dave approached it. They bumped into each other.

"Mama! Mama!" Dave shouted, lifting his mother into the air. *"The Italians are coming!"*

"What's the matter?" Dave's mother said.

"The Italians are coming to a race in Indianapolis," he shouted. "The team Cinzano!"

Dave was far too excited to hang around the house. The news that the Cinzano bicycle racing team was coming to Indianapolis was the most terrific thing that had ever happened to him. Maybe even more terrific than meeting the lovely Katherina.

He looked at the picture of the team again. Dressed all in black, they looked both noble and sinister. Roman gladiators must have looked like that, Dave thought.

The idea of not sharing this wonderful event with someone was unthinkable. He got on his bike and zoomed down the street, beaming with happiness. The dogs barked, and to him, it sounded like Italian music.

Then he saw the mailman, the man who was responsible for his being in possession of this splendid piece of information. It was only proper, Dave thought, that he should find a way to reward the man who had so illuminated his day.

He jumped the curb and came to a dead stop in front of the mailman, frightening the man nearly to death. The mailman was obviously unaware of Gimondi's renowned ability to stop on a dime.

Gimondi jumped off the bike and wrapped his arms around the mailman, enveloping him in a huge hug of gratitude. In the Italian style, he kissed the mailman on both cheeks.

"*Grazia, signor, molte grazia!*" he exclaimed, and jumped back on his bike and rode away, before the stunned mailman had a chance to reply.

Kissing the mailman wasn't enough for Dave. He wanted to do something really memorable. He wanted to share this great moment with someone who meant more to him than the mailman.

He was bicycling in downtown Bloomington when he saw the flower shop.

Perfetto!

He knew now how to celebrate this wonderful occasion. Smiling, he headed for the flower shop.

He was so full of himself and the wonderful news and his brilliant idea that he didn't notice that the girl who was waiting on him was the one who had been playing Frisbee that day with the lovely Katherina. Or perhaps he didn't recognize her, the lovely Katherina having cast a glow that dimmed everyone else around her by comparison.

The girl, whose name was Suzy, thrived on intrigue and complication. Not only that, she had a sort of a thing for Rod, and saw how she might cause a little trouble and turn a long-dormant situation to her advantage.

So, with a perfectly straight face she said, "You want the flowers to be sent to Katherine Maxwell."

"Yes."

"What's the address?" Suzy asked. She thought she recognized Dave now. He was one of the cutters in the car that ran over the Frisbee, who had almost got beaten up by Rod and her boyfriend.

Dave tried to fake it. "Sh . . . She's in a sorority . . . on Third Street."

"There's a lot of sororities there," she said, pretending to be helpful. "Phi Beta Phi, Kappa Kappa Gamma, Alpha Phi."

The recitation had the desired result. Dave looked very intimidated. He obviously had no idea what she was talking about.

But he tried to explain what he had seen in his simple cutter way: "It said on the front of the house . . . it had . . ." He drew designs in the air, "X, triangle, triangle."

Suzy decided he had suffered enough: "The Chi Delt house, eh?"

Gimondi was ecstatic. "Ah, yes! Chi-Delt, Chi-Delt." He repeated the words again, listening to the wonderful sound they made.

Chi-Delt. It was where she lived.

Dave came out of the flower shop, still floating on the cloud of his wonderful new information. Katherine Maxwell. Chi-Delt. A person could do anything in the world with that much information at his disposal.

And then his bubble burst, because Mike came driving by in his car at just that moment. When he saw Dave coming out of the flower shop, he stopped. Dave looked in the car. Cyril and Moocher were in there. All the boys. Everybody except himself.

"What were you doing in there?" Mike asked.

To Dave, it sounded like Mike was *accusing* him of something—accusing him of sending flowers to a girl.

He fumbled a bit over the answer. "Eh . . . I . . . I sent some flowers to the Chi-Delt . . ."

and then he hastily amended that . . . "to my mother." And then he changed the subject entirely. "Guess what! The Italians are coming."

"Guess what?" Mike countered. "Moocher's going."

Dave had no idea in the world what Mike was talking about.

Cyril leaned his head out of the car and said, "Talk to him, Dave."

Dave got on his bike and pedaled along beside Mike's slowly moving car.

"Where you going, Mooch?" he asked.

Cyril answered for Mooch: "He's getting a job." And as if that weren't revelation enough, he added, for emphasis, "Yes, a job!"

He said it the way you would say that a buddy was missing in action.

It took several more blocks before Dave found out what the job was. The guys had avoided the topic all the way through downtown Bloomington. But the car finally stopped at a place called Campus Car Wash. Moocher had taken a job at Campus Car Wash. Why it wasn't situated directly next to Campus Cars, Dave would never know. It would make more sense that way. Sell 'em and wash 'em.

Moocher had got out of the car. Cyril, still inside, had hold of his arm. Moocher was trying to shake free, trying to get on the job.

"Campus Car Wash," Mike said with contempt. "It's campus everything. I feel like some outcast surrounded by Disneyland."

And then he said what had been bothering him all along, what he hadn't been able to bring himself to say until now: "I thought we were going to stick together."

61

"I need a job, Mike," Moocher said, and shook himself free of Cyril's arm. He started walking over to Campus Car Wash. He was thinking about Nancy.

"Don't go, Mooch!" Cyril hollered after him. "They only let you out on weekends and national holidays!"

"Don't forget to write," Mike yelled out.

Moocher, feeling betrayed although he didn't really know why, headed toward the car wash, toward respectability, and enough money to do the things that he and Nancy had talked about when he had walked her back to work.

A bunch of college kids were already at work washing cars, looking very industrious, busy earning extra money that their parents could no doubt afford to give them if their parents weren't intent on making the college kids learn "character."

The owner of the establishment, a big man with a roll of fat over his belly, decided to let Moocher know what was what right off the bat.

"You're a little late," he said, "but I guess you won't let it happen again." He shoved some stuff at Moocher, and pointed. "Here's your sponge and here's your rag and there's your place."

Moocher was sure the guys had heard. He didn't look, he didn't want to look, but there was just no way they could not have heard.

He kept his cool. He wanted this job, for Nancy. For what it would mean to them. He took the sponge and the rag that the man had shoved at him and headed for the car wash area.

He passed something that looked to him

like it might be a time clock. He had never seen one before, but he had heard of them, and he imagined that was what they looked like. He ignored it—pretended he didn't see it—and that was when the trouble really started.

Because the guy with the big belly hollered after him, "Don't forget to punch the time clock, Shorty."

There were a lot of things you didn't do. You didn't cheat on your buddies, you didn't talk about a girl if you really cared about her, you didn't go back on your word. But most of all, you didn't call Moocher "Shorty."

So Moocher simply did as he was told. He turned around, very slowly and calmly. He took the rag the owner had handed him and wrapped it around his fist.

And then he punched the time clock.

Literally.

He gave it his best shot. He dealt it a death blow. He knocked the time clock off the wall. He watched it fall and spatter on the ground.

Then, with the calm, confident gaze of a willing worker who has simply done what he has been told to do, he looked over at the now apoplectic owner and said, "How's that?"

He didn't wait for the answer. He tossed the sponge aside and walked off the car wash lot, shaking the pain away from his fist.

But he somehow missed his moment of triumph. When he walked back to the curb, the guys weren't there. That didn't seem right to him. He had done what he had done under their eyes, and—although he would not have admitted this to himself—for their approval. He had betrayed Nancy for them, in a way. For the gang. And they weren't even there.

Despondent, suddenly alone, he shoved his hands, one of which hurt badly, into his pockets and started on home alone, to that little two-room shack.

And then Mike's car showed up. And all the guys were in it. Everybody was cheering. Mike was blowing his horn.

Gratefully, Moocher got in the car to receive his hero's welcome.

5

Most of the time, unless there was something special to do, the college kids hung out at the Student Union in the evenings. It was right on campus, it was fixed up pretty nice, and there wasn't all that much to do in Bloomington, anyway. Besides, if you went to a joint in Bloomington, there were sure to be cutters around, spoiling things. And cutters wouldn't think of coming to the Student Union.

It was actually just a big coffee shop with a jukebox, and right now it was packed with kids doing all the latest dances, some of them working up some fine free-form moves. There were a lot of Little 500 T-shirts in the place.

Somebody at a table was saying, "The S.A.E.'s have their whole team back. They're all swimmers." "See that guy there," he pointed.

"That's Rod Sommers. He rode seventy laps last year in the Little 500."

A reply came back: "We had Mark Spitz in our fraternity, but he wouldn't ride. Who's the girl with Sommers?"

The speaker was talking about Katherine. Everyone at the table turned to look at Rod and Katherine, seated at the next table. They were certainly the perfect couple, the BMOC couple, Rod strong and lean and arrogant, all blond hair and gleaming teeth, and Katherine startlingly pretty. They seemed to be engaged in serious, intimate conversation. Fortunately for them, no one could hear what they were saying.

"Suzy says this guy's sent you flowers," Rod was saying.

"So what?" Kathy said heatedly. "You never sent me flowers."

Rod chose to ignore that. He didn't have to send a girl flowers. He took a girl out, let her be seen with him, and that was enough as far as he was concerned. There were a lot of girls who would do anything—*anything*—to be seen with Rod Sommers, and judging from the way Suzy had rushed to relay this choice bit of gossip to him, Suzy was one of them. She was no Kathy, maybe, but not half bad.

Rod decided the best defense was a good offense. "Who is he, Kathy?"

"Just some crazy guy I met." She felt Rod's anger, and responded to it. "I don't know what's on your mind."

"And what I want to know," Rod said, "is what's on your mind, Kath?"

She hit him almost before the sentence was out of his mouth—a good, swift, hard one smack across the chops.

His first reaction was to check if anyone had noticed.

The people at the next table had, and they would tell the story over coffee for the next several weeks. But Rod didn't notice them. He was looking at Suzy. She was smiling.

It was a smile of anticipation, but Rod, who was not accustomed to getting smacked across the mouth by a girl, was hardly in the best shape in the world at that moment to realize that. He thought Suzy was smiling because Kathy had given him what he deserved, and so he looked away.

Suzy started to walk out of the Student Union, putting a little extra sway into it, but she couldn't resist looking back to see if Rod was watching her leave.

He was. She gave him another smile, one that a cretin would have found difficult to misinterpret, but he looked away from her again. He couldn't face her.

Suzy understood, and she wasn't in any hurry. She had waited this long, she could wait a little while longer.

As she walked out, a song started up on the jukebox, about somebody who loved somebody else even though it meant pain and misery and nights alone and broken dates.

Dave came back from church, riding on his bicycle. He was dressed in his Sunday best, except that his pants were rolled up to keep from getting oil on them.

They had been singing hymns in church, "How I Need Thee" and "What a Friend We Have in Jesus," but Dave was full of the music of Italy. It was a nice day, a lovely day, the sun shining.

He stopped at an intersection and looked around, a cautious habit that had, among other things, made him a champion, and he saw Moocher and Nancy walking down the street together.

They looked nice. They looked like a couple. They looked so much like a couple that he wanted to join them and bask in their aura of being together. But he decided not to. They looked so happy together that he felt he might have been intruding. He rode off toward his house. He figured Moocher and Nancy were probably going to see her parents, who lived nearby.

Moocher had chucked his job, but Nancy was still sticking with him.

That was nice.

Mrs. Stohler had capitulated to her husband's undeniable stress and frustration, and was making him french fries. Mr. Stohler was sitting in the kitchen, watching his wife, but what he was really doing, and what was driving him crazy, was listening to the sounds of happy Italian music coming from his son's room. Mr. Stohler needed to be soothed in some way, and maybe the french fries would do it. The way his wife made them, long and crisp, he could practically inhale them, suck them right down the gullet without chewing. They were better than a baby's bottle.

"I want an answer, Evelyn," Mr. Stohler said, even though he had not asked a question. "What're we going to do with him?"

"I don't know, dear," Mrs. Stohler said, putting the french fries on some toweling so they would have a little less cholesterol when they reached her husband's stomach. "I suppose we could strangle him while he's asleep."

"That's not funny, Evelyn," Mr. Stohler said.

Mrs. Stohler didn't think it was funny, either. She was simply giving voice to a course of action that she thought might occur to her husband some night when he was lying awake staring at the ceiling.

"Why don't you talk to him," she said, figuring it was better for her husband to talk to their son than strangle him.

"I'm afraid to talk to him," Mr. Stohler said. "I'm afraid to look at him. I'm afraid if I did, I'd see his eyes twirling like pinwheels."

Setting the plate down, Mrs. Stohler said, "The only reason I'm giving you these french fries is because you promised to calm down. Don't expect to get them again."

Mr. Stohler, already upset by the music coming from upstairs, was even more upset by the possibility that he might be receiving his final plate of french fries. This was a further injury. He decided it was his son's fault.

"I can't eat while that noise is going on," he sputtered, and got up from the table and headed for his son's room.

Mrs. Stohler prayed. Here was her husband setting off on a journey of mayhem again, and this time, he just might not be dissuaded. He was obviously getting desperate.

Dave didn't help matters any. Just at this moment, he appeared in the kitchen, resplendent in his Italian biking gear. It was like waving a red flag in front of a bull.

Mrs. Stohler decided the best thing she could do was wash the pan she had been cooking the french fries in. While she busied herself with that, pretending to notice nothing, her husband walked past their son and on out of the room.

Which left Dave standing there in the middle of the kitchen, looking at a plate of french fries on the table, obviously fresh, obviously tasty, and no one there to eat them. He sat down at the kitchen table and started shoving the french fries into his mouth.

In the other room, the Italian music stopped playing.

Mrs. Stohler was on the point of telling her son that she thought, in the circumstances, that eating the french fries was not the wisest thing in the world to do, when her husband suddenly reappeared at the door to the kitchen, and saw, with his own eyes, the latest way in which his son had contrived to torment him.

"Stop!" Mr. Stohler shouted, in a tone more suited to halting an army. "Them's my french fries!"

But he was too late. The french fries were gone, sucked down Dave's gullet like spaghetti.

Dave looked at his father, then at his mother, and then clutched his heart.

"Oh, Mama," he moaned, as if he were about to expire.

His mother was scared. The doctor had drilled her thoroughly on the harmful effects of french fries.

"Oh, dear," she cried out. "What's the matter?"

"My heart, Mama," Dave said. And then,

just in case she hadn't understood, he added, from the Italian phrase book, *"Mio cuoro!"*

Mrs. Stohler's worst suspicions were confirmed. "It's his heart," she said. "It's those french fries he ate."

Mr. Stohler was more concerned with property rights than personal illness. "Those were my french fries," he said.

But then Dave surprised them both. "I am in love, Mama, Papa," he said.

Mr. Stohler looked so nonplussed that Dave went to comfort him. "Papa," he said hugging his father with great affection. "I have such a pain in my heart," he turned and headed out of the kitchen in a daze.

Mr. Stohler walked over to the kitchen table and looked at the empty plate. His desolation knew no boundaries.

To his surprise, his wife went to the refrigerator and started emptying food into the plastic baggie in her hand: the Italian food went first, the cheeses and the sausage, but she followed that with what eggs remained in the dozen-egg container, and half a rasher of bacon.

Mr. Stohler didn't know what his wife was up to.

"What are you doing?" he asked her.

She continued what she was doing, so he called her by name: "Evelyn."

"I won't have any heart attack food in my house," she answered. "That was a warning to us. If anybody dies around here, it won't be on my conscience."

She put an unopened jar of olives stuffed with pimento into the bulging baggie.

Mr. Stohler didn't quite understand, so he said it again: "What are you doing, Evelyn?"

"These are all the foods the doctor said you can't have," Mrs. Stohler said, "and they're going out."

Mr. Stohler watched his wife. He tried not to scream. He hated waste, even of Italian food.

"I'm having a nightmare," he said.

Dave was way out in the country, riding his bike. He wasn't riding very hard. In fact, both his hands were off the handlebars. One held his Italian phrase book, which he was studying. With the other, he was combing his hair back, trying to make it look more like the hair of the members of the team Cinzano.

The further out in the country he got, the faster he rode. Being away from town seemed to free him, allowed him to go faster. He looked up at the birds perched on the telephone wires. It seemed to him that they looked like notes on a musical staff, and he tried to hum the melody they made. Soon he was Gimondi singing a Neopolitan melody.

Sometime later, he was facing back the way he had come, back toward town. He put the phrase book away. He began to hyperventilate. A hard, competitor's look came into his eye. He looked at his wristwatch.

He seemed to be waiting for something.

He was at a place where a country dirt road joined the highway. A nearby sign read: BLOOMINGTON—50 MILES. He looked at his watch again, then pedaled out onto the highway. Right on time, a big Fruehauf trailer truck came around the turn and barreled down the highway.

As the truck passed, a big smile formed on Dave's face. He could see the big logo on the side of the truck as it sped past: CINZANO.

But to Dave, it wasn't a Cinzano truck, it was the *team* Cinzano, and he, Gimondi, would beat them.

He speeded up and got directly behind the truck, getting into the slipstream, letting the truck's air pocket carry him along.

The driver, seeing what Dave had done, speeded up and shifted gears.

Dave, in the slipstream, also shifted gears.

The driver of the Cinzano truck looked at his speedometer. He was doing forty. He looked at his side mirror and saw Dave, still behind him. He stuck out four fingers and stepped on the gas.

When he had the truck up to fifty, he looked again, and, to his surprise, the kid was still there, pedaling away. He stuck out five fingers and shifted gears again.

Dave shifted into his highest gear and poured it on. He was going all out now. Pulled along by the slipstream and his own momentum, he was going faster on a bike than he had ever gone in his life.

The truckdriver looked at his speedometer. He had it up to sixty now. He looked in his side mirror again. The kid was still back there. Amazing.

Then he saw something else in the mirror. A flashing red light. An instant later, he heard the wail of the state trooper's siren.

Dave was so intent on keeping his momentum up, that it was a moment before he noticed he had to work harder to keep his speed, and another moment before he realized the Cinzano truck wasn't in front of him any more. He looked over his shoulder and saw the trooper talking to the driver at the side of the road. Wow, he thought. He had won, by a technicality. He had beat the Cinzano team on a foul. He kept going.

Pain was beginning to distort his face. Sweat dripped down his chin, poured down his sides, dripped onto the highway. But his legs kept on moving in the same rhythmical motion.

He got a moment's respite, coasting down a hill, and then had to pump extra hard to get back up the incline.

He kept on going.

He was going to do the whole fifty miles, truck or no truck.

When he was nearing the 50-mile mark he started to sprint, his face nearly ripped apart in agony. He looked like an astronaut in a wind tunnel, taking a stress test.

He passed a highway sign: WELCOME TO BLOOMINGTON. HOME OF INDIANA UNIVERSITY.

As he passed the sign, Dave looked at his watch. Not a bad time. Not bad at all. He was elated. A huge grin split his salt-covered face. He reached for his water bottle and sprayed it over his head as if it were a bottle of victory champagne.

6

Mike was telling the guys about Wyoming again. He was sitting on the sidewalk with Cyril and Moocher out in front of the café where Nancy worked. He had a magazine in his hands, with the Marlboro Man on the back cover. The Marlboro Man looked pretty impressive, with his mustache and his Clint Eastwood steely gaze and his hairy hand with the tattoo on the back. And the scenery around him looked pretty impressive, too.

"That's the place to be," Mike said, tapping the magazine with a finger. "Wyoming. Look at that . . . prairies and mountains and nobody around. All you need is a bedroll and a good horse."

Mike could see himself lying out under the stars, with nobody bugging him.

"Don't forget your toothbrush," Cyril reminded him. "You're still in your cavity-prone years."

You're an idiot, Cyril, Mike thought, but he didn't say it, because he wanted Cyril to come with him to Wyoming.

A campus police black-and-white pulled up in front of them.

A big, beefy guy in suntans got out, a blond guy going bald in his late twenties, with the beginnings of a truly remarkable gut spreading over his wide belt.

The campus cop approached them, hitching up his pants.

Mike put a cigarette in his mouth.

"Here comes your brother," Moocher said to Mike.

"I hear you've been hot-rodding through the campus again," Mike's brother said to him.

"I was just . . ." Mike started to say, but he never got it out, because his brother rode right over him.

"I'll take the car back if you keep it up," Mike's brother snapped.

"All right, all right," Mike said. There were some threats you just couldn't do anything about.

Mike's brother started past them, going toward the café to get something to eat. He was thinking about a double cheeseburger. He nodded at Moocher and Cyril and said, "How you doing, guys?" and walked on past.

"We're a little disturbed by the developments in the Middle East," Cyril said to Mike's brother's back, "but other than that . . ."

His brother gone, Mike started acting tough

again. He always seemed three or four years younger when his brother was around.

"Campus cop," Mike said viciously.

It was still daytime, but dark enough to be night. The sky was black, and the rain was coming down. Mr. Stohler stood in the doorway of his office, more relaxed than he had been in a long time. Nobody would come in weather like this. For once, he didn't mind. He could use a little time to himself, a little time without pressure. Time to think. Time to get things sorted out. He looked at his spreading pot and sucked it in. But it didn't stay in. As soon as he let his breath out, there it was again. Like all his other troubles.

Moocher was helping Nancy move into her new place. The rain didn't make things any easier. Moocher was carrying a huge chest of drawers across the sidewalk. The chest of drawers was nearly as big as he was.

Nancy looked worried about him.

"I'm fine, I'm fine," Moocher said, puffing away.

"You're so strong," Nancy said.

As Moocher continued on his way with the big chest, one of the drawers slipped out, causing Nancy's clothes to scatter on the sidewalk.

Nancy kneeled down and picked up the clothes, putting them back in the drawer. As she picked up a long, pretty dress, she held it up in front of her jeans.

"You know what?" Nancy said.

"No, what?"

"I'm thinking of getting my hair done."

She pushed her hair back in a classic way.

"I thought maybe something like this," Nancy said. "What do you think?"

Moocher thought the new hairstyle made her look lovely. He thought about how she would look in the dress with her hair like that.

"Not bad," Moocher said.

When it seemed certain that the rain wasn't going to let up, Mr. Stohler took one of the fanciest cars on the lot, an old Lincoln that the college kids would think was a classic, and drove out to the quarry shop. Even though it was hot inside the car, and he was sweating, he had his tie and jacket on—even a hat. He wanted to look good.

He pulled into the parking lot and got out. Coming here was like coming home. He heard the sound of machinery from inside the huge building. It made him remember all the days he had spent inside this place, shouting over the incredible noise every time he wanted to say something to the fellow next to him. Whenever he thought about this place, his throat felt rough.

The noise got louder as he walked toward the building. He tried to avoid stepping into the limestone dust—he had just given himself a shoeshine—but the dust was everywhere. That was how you told a cutter. No matter how often he showered or took a bath, he could never get all the dust off him.

Several cutters sat around on boxes at

the entrance of the shop, eating their lunch out of paper bags. The noise didn't seem to bother them any more than the dust that was getting into their sandwiches. One of them looked up and saw Mr. Stohler.

"Well," the cutter said. "Look who's back."

Mr. Stohler smiled and gave an elaborate wave. He was glad to be there, but he was, at the same time, trying to keep his distance a little, to show them how far he had come from this beginning. His suit and tie and hat made him look like a visiting politician, come to ask the factory workers for votes on their lunch hour.

"Well, if you don't look like one of them government safety inspectors," one of the cutters said, bursting Mr. Stohler's bubble.

"No," another cutter said. "A union organizer."

They all laughed then, and got up to shake hands with him. Except for one of the younger men, who remained in his seat eating his sandwich. The cutters slapped Mr. Stohler on the back with their dusty hands, leaving prints all over his jacket.

"We'll start you as an apprentice again," one of them said.

"Oh no, you won't," Mr. Stohler said, joshing right back. "I'm just visiting. But if I wanted to come back I could pick up where I left off."

He thought he could, at that. And at the moment, he wanted to find out. The entrance of the shop drew him like a magnet. He started to go inside. A couple of the fellows went with him, and he took half a sandwich from one of them. The old instincts were coming back. He felt as if he was going back inside to get going on a piece of work he had been doing an hour ago.

The young cutter who was still eating his sandwich looked up and said to the fellow next to him, "Who's he?"

Mr. Stohler heard him, and looked back over his shoulder. The remark hurt. It was like going back to your old house and finding somebody else living there who didn't know who you were.

He felt better once he got inside. The noise was deafening, and you could barely make out the shapes of the men through the dust. But when they saw him coming, they stopped what they were doing long enough to smile and wave at him. These fellows knew who he was, all right.

He watched the electric saws move back and forth in a hypnotic way, cutting into the huge blocks of stone. He saw the water coming down to cool the blades. The sight brought everything back.

He took off his coat, draping his jacket over a big wooden chair.

He drove wooden wedges into a cut block of limestone. The physical work, though unaccustomed, felt good to him. Water fell on him. Sweat poured off him. An old-timer who had lost his teeth a long time ago watched him, grinning with his gums. Mr. Stohler looked like a fountain. You couldn't tell what was pouring off him, sweat or the water from overhead. He didn't care. He was having the best time he'd had in far too long.

He watched the circular saws spinning enormous limestone columns, chisels indenting grooves in them, making them look Greek: Ionic, Doric, Corinthian. They could do anything you wanted, right here in this quarry shop. It had been good to be part of it.

Mr. Stohler worked on his block of limestone until he was tired and out of breath. That had happened sooner than he had expected. Maybe he should try to get in shape, after all, he thought. It did a man good to do physical work like this. There was a dignity to it, more dignity than trying to sell clunkers to kids in cashmere sweaters.

He bummed a cigarette off a cutter and lit it. The man moved on to his place. Mr. Stohler watched him, smoking the cigarette. He liked being here. He liked it just fine.

A man shouted something at him. Mr. Stohler couldn't make it out. He cupped his hand over his ear to signal that he hadn't heard.

The man shouted again over the din: "YOUR SON. HOW'S YOUR SON DOING?"

"FINE," Mr. Stohler shouted back. "JUST FINE." He wanted the man to think that everything was going well with him. That meant with Dave, too.

"THAT'S MINE OVER THERE," the man shouted, and pointed.

Mr. Stohler followed the direction of the man's finger with his eyes. The man was pointing at the young fellow who had asked who Mr. Stohler was.

Mr. Stohler sat down in the chair that had his coat draped over it. In his younger days, he had sat many times in this same chair. He felt the notches in the armrest. His fingers knew right where to go, just as they knew what to do with the tools he had been using. He picked up a piece of limestone lying by the chair. That felt familiar, too. Then he looked around again.

He wanted to look at the place one more time before he had to leave.

The rain was pouring down, but Dave was pumping away on his bike, just the same. But not quite riding. He had his bike up on "rollers," a stationary device that locked his bike in place and allowed him to get in some practice. Something like an Exercycle. He was outside, on the porch. It felt good to be outside in the rain, breathing the clean air, making his legs stronger.

He looked up and saw Cyril running through the rain toward him. Cyril was wearing a yellow rubber rain cape and carrying a guitar.

A little later, Mrs. Stohler was mopping the kitchen floor. She could hear the sound of Enrico Gimondi coming from her son's room. She could hear the sound of Cyril's guitar, trying to pick out the sweet Italian melody. She stopped her mopping to listen. There was a look of romantic yearning in her eyes.

Up in Dave's room, the phonograph was turned off now. Cyril, concentrating intensely, his tongue sticking out between his teeth, was trying to work out the melody Gimondi had been singing. It didn't go too well at first, but as he kept at it, it got better, and by the time he started to play it again, he was smiling.

Dave was smiling, too. He was sitting on his bed, wearing a hairnet, trying to coerce his curly hair into the straight, sleek style of the team Cinzano.

"That's it!" he said happily. "That's the song, Cyril. I recognize it."

"Yeah," Cyril said, an artist receiving his just due.

"Only you'll have to make it louder," Dave said. "Real loud."

"Don't worry," Cyril said. "I'll make this catgut meow."

Fellini, formerly Jake, left the room and ran out of the house. Mr. Stohler, who had just got out of his car and was running through the rain to the house, almost collided with the cat, but he was even more startled at what confronted him once he got inside.

His wife, inspired by Enrico Gimondi and Cyril, had done a little cosmetic work on herself, her cheeks now red with rouge, her eyelids frosted blue. She looked quite pretty, in fact.

Mr. Stohler felt he had to say something, but direct compliments were hardly his style. "You . . . eh . . . you waxed the floor, eh?" he said finally. "Looks nice."

Mrs. Stohler smiled her thanks. She knew her husband well and knew what he really meant.

A little later, Dave and Cyril slipped out of the house. They were riding double on the bike, really covering ground. Cyril was carrying his guitar. They were fully prepared now. They were on a mission of great urgency and importance.

Mr. Stohler thought he had had all the surprises a person could be expected to stand in one evening, but there was more to come.

Here he was, seated at the dinner table, chomping on a carrot stick. But that was not what was the matter. He had expected carrot sticks. What he hadn't expected was candles on the table; or the dining-room table, for that matter, the table only used for company; with a gleaming white cloth on it, and the candles lit, like they were in some fancy French restaurant in Indianapolis. He thought it was a plot to make him forget he was eating carrot sticks.

But if his wife were part of a scheme with the doctor to make carrot sticks more palatable, she wouldn't be dolled up in a dress, with stuff on her face bought from the Avon lady. Mr. Stohler couldn't figure it out.

Then Mrs. Stohler threw him a curve. She got up from the table and said, "How about . . ." And just when Mr. Stohler was sure the next words out of her mouth would be "some nice broccoli," she said instead, "How about a little music?"

Dave and Cyril had biked over to the Chi Delt house. They had parked the bike in the big parking lot. It was a lovely night, clear and cool after the rain, perfect for what they had come to do.

Cyril leaned against a tree, just off the stone path that led to the Chi Delt house. His guitar was at the ready. Dave was farther away, closer to the parking lot, ready to beat a hasty retreat should his idea not work out the way he intended.

He took a deep breath, hyperventilating as he would before an important race, and nodded to Cyril.

Cyril started to play. He sounded very good, very soulful.

Dave stepped out of the shadows, looked up at the darkened windows of the Chi Delt house, and called out, in his loudest voice and finest Italian accent, "KA-THE-RI-NA!"

Upstairs, a couple of lights went on.

At Dave's house, Mrs. Stohler had put on some music for her husband and herself, to make the dinner more pleasant. She had picked Enrico Gimondi's album, which she had taken from her son's room upstairs. Enrico Gimondi smiled up at her from the album cover.

The song Gimondi was singing to Mr. and Mrs. Stohler was the same song Cyril was playing in the shadows in front of the Chi Delt house, the song he had worked on so hard all afternoon.

He finished his elaborate introduction, and nodded at Dave. It was Dave's moment to appear. He stepped out of the shadows to stand in the pool of light made by the street light on the stone path, and he sang the words of

Enrico Gimondi with heart and fervor, sang them with as much feeling as Mario Lanza singing to Kathryn Grayson.

Several girls came to the window. They wanted to see what was going on. Serenades were old-fashioned—they had gone out in the Fifties—and even then, they were never sung in Italian. So this was an event.

One of the girls who came to the window was Katherine. Dave recognized her the minute she appeared in the light. She eclipsed the others. Then more girls came to the window, crowding in behind her.

Enrico Gimondi began to sing with greater purpose, and ever more elaborate gestures.

Surrounded by her girlfriends, her sorority sisters, Katherine felt obliged to look upon what was going on in her behalf as corny and silly. But the more she listened to the young man singing to her from down below, his arms stretched upward toward her, the less she felt like mocking what was going on.

From where he was, down there in the street, Dave could see Katherine's lovely face change slightly. He could see that she was fighting her feelings, trying to preserve her detachment.

And he could see that her girlfriends had quieted down and were starting to listen. He even thought they seemed jealous of Katherine.

What Dave couldn't see was Suzy, the girl who had sold him the flowers, standing a bit apart from the group, trying to think of what she might do to turn this new development to her advantage.

Cyril was oblivious to everything but his music. He hunched over his guitar, intent on his new-found virtuosity, sweating like an old Mississippi blues player. He hit one little lick that pleased him very much, and so he complimented himself: "Play it, Cyril!" he shouted.

Mrs. Stohler came back to the table, having put Gimondi's record on. She smiled down at her husband, hoping for approval, hoping for romance. Mr. Stohler was not as happy as she had hoped he would be.

She had forgotten, in her romantic fantasy, what the music of Gimondi had come to mean to her husband, what symbolic value the singer had in this house.

Mr. Stohler had a carrot in his hand. He was holding it aloft, like a baton. As Gimondi's voice sang out, Mr. Stohler looked at the carrot as though he wanted to assassinate it.

Suzy was out in the hall of the sorority house, on the pay phone, having aced out three girls who had insisted the line be kept clear because their boyfriends were going to call. Suzy didn't care about that. She detested the way her sorority sisters hung around the phone, waiting for calls. She had figured out, fairly early on in life, that the secret was to make outgoing calls and let the incoming calls come in as they might.

Right now, she was making a very important outgoing call, transmitting information, planting another time bomb and waiting to see if it would explode.

Rod finally came on the line. His frat brother had answered the phone, then hollered down the hall, and now here *he* was, a little bit surprised that it was Suzy calling him, and not Kathy.

"Oh, hi, Rod," Suzy said when he came on the line. She was playing it real cool, working a little double shuffle, making it seem as though it was actually Rod who had called her up.

Rod was brusque with her, demanding to know why she had pulled him out of his poker game, so she laid it right on him: "I was just wondering if you knew that there was a guy here serenading Kath."

His response was everything she could have wished for.

Dave was still in front of the sorority house, singing away. He looked up at the window, and there was the beautiful Katherina, leaning out. The expression on her face had changed. She was charmed now, she was completely won over. She didn't think it was corny any more. She thought that a serenade was a terrific thing for a guy to want to do for her.

She leaned down out of the window and smiled. The smile lit up the night for Dave, and he basked in the glow of it.

Behind Katherine, Suzy moved up to the window. "Hi, Kath, what's going on?" she said sweetly.

Rod felt his rightful territory had been invaded. He persuaded several of his frat brothers to come help him. They charged out of the frat house and piled into Rod's Mercedes convertible.

Dave had finished his song, and had so won over the girls in the window that several of them were applauding. The lovely Katherina was not among them. She had disappeared from the window moments before.

Dave wasn't worried. He thought he knew where she had gone and hoped that he was right.

At that moment, Katherine appeared before him. The beautiful princess had come down from her tower, and was now speaking directly to the serenader, thanking him for his song.

And now she was on the back of his bike, as they sped away from the campus, her lovely arms wrapped around him as he pedaled as far away from the sorority house as he could possibly get. She was no longer the unattainable maiden, but a girl hugging his back and ready to go with him wherever he might go.

Ready to go with him to the ends of the earth.

Cyril watched the pair ride away. He had done his job. He had been a craftsman. He had been amply rewarded.

Rod came driving slowly up the street behind the wheel of his Mercedes convertible, his head out the window, scanning the dark streets. He spotted a guy walking along strumming the guitar, headed toward the parking lot.

A guy with a guitar was obviously a serenader, Rod reasoned. This is the jerk they were going to get.

"That must be him," Rod said to his car full of fraternity brothers.

He hit the brakes.

Cyril heard the sound of a car door slamming and looked over in the direction of the noise. He saw a bunch of guys rushing out of a car, headed in his direction.

"Ooops," Cyril said. "If I were a cartoon, I'd go: HELP. And you'd see my tonsils wiggling in the back."

Cyril started to run. Rod and his pals came running across the lawn, right after him.

Dave and Katherine returned to the Chi Delt house. Dave was in heaven. He felt he'd been riding on the wind.

Katherine took her arms from around Dave's waist and started to get off the bike. They looked at each other for a moment, not knowing what to say.

"I have to go in," Katherine said finally.

"*Buono notte*, Katherina," Enrico said.

She smiled sweetly at him. "I haven't ridden double since I was a small girl, and I've never been serenaded. So, it was a lovely evening." Then, with a slight, deprecating gesture, she added, "*Molte grazia.*"

She seemed a little embarrassed by her Italian, so Enrico Gimondi grandly gestured to her that she hadn't done too badly.

Then she leaned over and kissed him,

very sweetly, and Dave felt far greater than Enrico Gimondi could even have dreamed of being.

Later, try as he might, Dave was never able to remember the ride home.

7

Cyril looked terrible. He looked like somebody had taken a hammer to him. But he wouldn't talk about it.

He was walking with the guys, down by the railroad tracks, sipping a Coke. His lips were split, so it hurt him to drink. Parts of his face were interesting shades of yellow and purple.

"He won't tell me who did it," Mike said.

"It was dark," Cyril said. "All I can tell you for sure is that they all wore Brut aftershave and smelled of Lavoris."

"What were you doing there by yourself?" Mike asked him.

Cyril looked at Dave, and Dave looked at Cyril, and Cyril said, "Just walking."

"What kind of car did they drive?" Mike asked. He didn't want to let it alone.

"It was this Mercedes convertible," Cyril said reluctantly.

"I've seen that car," Mike said, clenching his fists. Sure he had. It belonged to that high-diving college kid who thought he was such hot stuff.

"All right," Mike said. "They want to fight ... we'll give them a fight."

Cyril didn't like that idea at all. He had already been in one fight with those guys, and he was not anxious to repeat the experience.

"Chief Mike plenty brave," Cyril said, in his best Hollywood manner, "but I say this: We rednecks are few. Paleface college students are many. I counsel peace."

Mike grabbed Cyril by the shirt. He wasn't going to let that snotty college kid get away, not when he had a legitimate reason to lay him out. "C'mon," he said to the guys. "Let's find him."

Cyril felt Mike's urgency had nothing to do with avenging the beating. He saw a trash can, and hook-shot the Coke bottle at it. It went right in, not touching any of the rim, and broke with a satisfying crash. Two points.

Cyril smiled. That was his idea of violence.

But, as usual, Mike had his way. The guys piled into his car and rode off toward the campus, looking for the guy in the Mercedes convertible. That is, Mike was looking for him, and the other guys were pretending to look for him.

Mike parked the car by a grassy field.

The plan was to sit on the grass, watching cars go by, and when Cyril recognized the Mercedes convertible or some of the guys who had beat him up, he would holler out, and then the guys would go after them.

A group of college kids got together on the field for a football game. The guys sat and watched the game, and at first concentrated on spotting Cyril's attackers. Before long, however, they were engrossed in the game.

Especially Mike. He followed the plays with complete interest, making little body movements as if he were on the field himself.

Before they realized it, it was getting dark and the game was over and the college kids were splitting up into little groups and going home.

Mike was angry. He picked up a stick and threw it.

"I really thought I was a great quarterback in high school," he said. "I still think so. I can't even bring myself to light a cigarette, 'cause I keep thinking I should stay in shape. And you know what gets me?" The anger crept into his voice. "Living here and reading in the papers how some hotshot kid is the new star on the college team. Every year there'll be a new one, and it's never going to be me."

The guys were embarrassed. But Mike didn't notice their embarrassment. He was caught up in his confession.

"I'll just be Mike," he said. "Twenty-year-old Mike. Thirty-year-old Mike." His voice got more intense: "*Old mean old man Mike.* But the college kids will never get old . . . out of shape . . . 'cause new ones keep coming every year. And they'll keep callin' us 'cutters.' "

. And then he said the worst thing of all. "To them it's a dirty word, but to me it'll just be something else I never got a chance to be."

He stopped talking and stared into space. He took out a cigarette and stuck it in his mouth, as if acknowledging that it didn't matter whether he stayed in shape or not. The guys looked at him with sympathy and understanding, but Mike didn't want their sympathy and understanding. He got in his car and started it up. He had forgotten all about the guys that beat up on, Cyril.

Cyril and Moocher got into the car, looking as though they'd rather be anywhere else in the world.

Dave hung back. "I have to go somewhere," he said.

Dave didn't want to tell the guys he was going to meet Katherine. Cyril knew about her, of course, but even Cyril didn't know the whole story. And, grateful as he was to Cyril for providing the guitar accompaniment that had led to the most wonderful night of his life, Dave couldn't reveal his true feelings.

Nor could he introduce Katherine to his friends. He would have liked to, and he would have enjoyed the expression on the guys' faces when they saw him with a girl like Katherine, but that was impossible, of course. Because Katherine thought he was Enrico Gimondi, from Naples, Italy.

He didn't like to think of what might happen if Katherine found out he was lying to her.

But for now Enrico Gimondi was walking with the lovely Katherina on the campus at dusk, and she was questioning him about his home.

"I've never been to Naples," she said, "but it sounds lovely."

"Oh, *Napoli*," Enrico said. "*Sì, signorina*. So beautiful. We live by the sea. My papa, he he has a boat . . . a fisherman." He was caught up in his own improvisation, and decided a fisherman would probably have a big family. "My mama, she has ten *bambini* . . . and I am eleven." For a moment, he panicked, worried that she would ask him the names of his ten brothers and sisters. Fortunately, Katherine just smiled compassionately. "And when I left for America," he continued quickly, "they all cry big tears. . . ."

The scene moved him so much he became poetic: "Tears like big figs . . ."

Katherine took a little book out of her bag and showed it to him.

"Look what I bought," she said. "I figured I might as well learn a little."

Dave stared at the book. It was the same Italian phrase book that he had.

He suffered conflicting emotions. First, his heart soared with joy—she had bought an Italian phrase book! She wanted to know him better, to enter his world, to be part of his life! But on the other hand, she was older than he, and very possibly smarter, and who knew how long it would be before she knew more Italian than he did?

Gimondi make a gesture of dismissal. "You never learn Italian from that book," he said. "I know that book. No good."

They walked down the campus, toward the Student Union.

Elsewhere on campus, Rod was driving along in his Mercedes convertible with the Texas plates. A blond was with him. She was a freshman, new on campus. If you asked Rod, she was the pick of the whole freshman class. A lot of guys had tried to hustle her for a date, but Rod never had much trouble acing other guys out when he saw a girl he wanted to date.

He was going to take the girl to the Student Union, where people who knew both him and Kath were sure to be. Wait till Kath heard he was with a girl who looked like this one. When Kath heard about this, she'd drop that guitar player so fast, the guy wouldn't know what had happened to him.

Rod tooled along with one hand on the wheel, the other casually slung over the seat. He gave the girl his best BMOC smile. "You haven't pledged any sorority yet?" he asked.

"No," she said.

"You should," Rod said, playing the older guy willing to give advice. "Most frat guys won't go out with dormies. I'm the exception."

"You're on the swimming team, eh?" the girl asked. She wasn't much for conversation.

"Yep," he told her. "Butterfly." He gave her another one of his smiles, cool and confident.

He was so intent on the freshman girl that he didn't notice when Mike came driving along in the other direction.

Mike noticed Rod though. This was what he'd been waiting for. He braked suddenly, shifted into reverse, and started going backwards down the street, parallel to the Mercedes.

Now Rod had to notice. A maniac was going backwards down the street beside him. Rod stared at Mike, who stared back.

"Is that him?" Mike said loudly.

"I guess," said Cyril from the back seat, but he didn't sound happy about it.

Mike shifted into first and waited for an opening.

"Who were they?" the blond asked Rod.

"A bunch of cutters," he said.

"What are cutters?"

"Townies," he said.

She didn't say anything. At least she was smart enough not to have to ask what townies were.

That ended their conversation until they got to the Union, where Rod pulled in and parked.

The Union was built in the shape of an L. The long section of the L was where most people usually sat, and where there was dancing, when anybody wanted to dance. That section was packed now, and there were a few couples dancing. The short section of the L was for recluses, people who went to the Union to study, or for independents, who weren't in a frat or sorority and therefore didn't know many people.

Dave and Katherine were sitting in the short section. Neither wanted to be seen, and besides, they wanted to be alone.

A waiter came up to them and asked for their order.

"*Due capuccino, por favore,*" Gimondi said.

Mike pulled into the Union parking lot and parked right next to the Mercedes with the Texas plates.

Cyril and Moocher seemed unwilling to get out of the car. They stared out the window, first at the Mercedes, then at the entrance to the Student Union. The entrance seemed forbidding to them, as if it should have a sign over it saying ABANDON ALL HOPE, YE WHO ENTER HERE.

"We can't go in there," Cyril said.

"Oh yeah?" Mike said, getting out of the car. "Watch this."

There was nothing for Cyril and Moocher to do but follow him.

A long stairway led up to the Union, and as they climbed the long flight of stairs, Cyril found himself wondering what was at the top. Probably a guillotine, he thought.

Rod was looking for a place where he and the blond freshman could sit down. The place was jammed. Not an empty table anywhere. For a minute, he was afraid he was going to have to sit in the short section of the L, otherwise known as Dormie Heaven, with the creepos. If that happened, the freshman girl wouldn't get to see what a wheel he was, with everybody coming up and saying hello to him. And his friends wouldn't get to see him with the blond, which would prevent them relaying the information back to Kath.

He was about to make the best of it and head to Dormie Heaven anyway, when somebody got up, and Rod made one of his smoothest moves. He grabbed the vacated table, acing three couples who had been waiting before him and watched with pleasure as the freshman moved into the seat opposite him.

Katherine and Dave were drinking their *capuccino* and talking about their home lives. That is to say, the lovely Katherina was talking about her home life, opening up in a way she hadn't done with a guy in a long time. Rod had never been interested. Enrico Gimondi, for his part, was improvising like crazy.

"It's kind of nice to hear of somebody who misses his parents," Katherine said.

Enrico Gimondi couldn't imagine it being any other way. "*Certo*, I miss," he said. "Just like you miss your mama and papa."

"I hardly miss them," she said. "I went as far as I could to get away from them."

Gimondi looked at her intently, wondering how this could possibly be true of such a lovely young girl. It depressed him, but as usual he found the bright side. That was one of his strengths.

"Ah," he said, "but they miss you, eh? At home, they sit and look at your picture. Ah, they are saying, how we miss our Katherina, our *bambina....*"

Gimondi was too caught up in his improvisation to notice that tears were forming in Katherine's eyes. He was assuming she had a loving, happy home life—something so far from her actual experience that it pained her to think about it.

Katherina took a cigarette and lighter out of her bag, hoping to divert attention from her tears.

As is widely known, a Continental gentleman of the stature of Enrico Gimondi does not allow a lady to light her own cigarette, whether or not he approves of the fact that she smokes. He gallantly took the lighter from her, only to find he didn't know how to use it. It was a fearsomely complicated thing, with all kinds of little brass knobs and wheels on it, and try as he might, he couldn't get the thing to work. He got desperate, and started to lose his cool.

Then, quite by accident, he stumbled on the right button to press down. But apparently, in his previous explorations, he had fiddled with the wrong wheels, because a huge jet of flame burst out and shot nearly up to the ceiling, scaring Dave to death.

He let go of the button, but it stuck, and the flame wouldn't go out. He blew on it, shook it, but it wouldn't go out.

Katherina started to laugh, which was intolerable.

So he poured coffee on the thing, and it went out, finally.

Katherine couldn't stop laughing.

Making a recovery from such a situation is what makes the Enrico Gimondis of the world a breed apart. "You shouldn't smoke," he said. "I go bring more coffee." He took their cups and headed toward the self-service cafeteria line, on the other side of the L.

• • •

Mike, Moocher, and Cyril stood in the entrance of the Union, wondering where to go and what to do. They were trying very hard to look tough, but they wouldn't have fooled a soul. They were lost and intimidated, and they looked it. Everyone they saw looked to them as though he or she had all the money in the world.

They were so busy scanning the terrain for the enemy that they didn't see Dave get on the end of the cafeteria line with two empty cups in his hand.

What they did see, though—Mike saw him first—was a guy who looked like Rod go into the bowling alley, which was off an exit about halfway down the long part of the L.

"There he is," Mike said, and the three of them headed for the bowling alley.

Rod was waiting on the cafeteria line, holding forth to a bunch of hero-worshippers who were hanging around waiting to catch whatever Rod might care to say to them. Rod was talking about bike racing, as if he knew something about it.

"The only way to train for bike racing," Rod was saying, "is what we do in swimming: interval training."

Dave, who was standing in line in back of Rod whom he didn't recognize, found it difficult to keep a straight face. He didn't want to laugh at the guy, but he found it impossible not to say what he thought. Interval training was an old concept. No one won races with it any more. "The Germans . . ." he said, trying not to laugh . . . "they use interval training and the Italians . . . they don't. The Italians," he continued, "they beat the pants off Germans."

Rod whirled around and glared at Dave with utter scorn. Who is this creep, Rod thought, not recognizing Dave.

But Dave recognized the guy he thought of now as Katherine's former boyfriend. He smiled to himself and turned to examine a cheese danish.

Mike, Cyril, and Moocher had followed the big blond guy they thought was Rod into the bowling alley. Now they were standing around fidgeting, not knowing how to make an approach.

Mike was telling himself that you didn't just fall on a guy from behind and start to beat him up, but he was having trouble coming up with a way to get things started.

Moocher and Cyril were hoping Mike would just forget the whole thing.

For lack of something better to do, Cyril walked over to the ball rack and stuck his fingers in the holes of one of the balls. When he tried to get his fingers out, he couldn't.

Cyril got out of the bowling alley as fast as he could. Mike and Moocher followed. Cyril still had his fingers stuck in the bowling ball, and was trying to hide the fact as best he could, but it's pretty hard to look casual when you are carrying a bowling ball around on the end of your finger.

"I can't get it off," he moaned.

He felt all the college kids were staring at him. They could see he was a cutter, who,

104

worse still, had a bowling ball attached to his finger.

Even Mike felt the stare. He was trying to be cool, but he wasn't succeeding.

"My finger can't breathe," Cyril said, swinging the bowling ball dangerously, sending Mike and Moocher scurrying out of his way.

Two coeds walked past, looking no doubt for a place to have coffee without being bothered by guys pestering them.

Cyril couldn't resist. "Hi," he said. "What's your major?"

The girls walked past him with the disdain the remark demanded.

Mike had rounded the corner by now, into the long part of the L.

"Looks like he left," Mike said. He sounded hopeful. They were all willing to take it on faith that Rod had left. They wanted nothing more than to get out of there.

As they walked toward the exit doors, Cyril, still carrying his bowling ball along like an unwanted appendage, saw this terrific-looking blond sitting by herself in a booth.

Again he couldn't restrain himself. Common sense told him to get out while he still had the chance, but he couldn't pass up the opportunity.

"Hi," he said to the blond, "what's your major?"

"Psych," she said, friendly as could be.

Rod showed up just at that moment, carrying a tray of drinks for himself and the blond who had just told Cyril what her major was.

Cyril saw Rod.

Mike saw Rod and Cyril.

Moocher, already halfway out the door,

105

resigned himself to the inevitable. Eminently practical, he wrapped a handkerchief around his fist.

Cyril cringed. He could feel the forth-coming blows on his body as clearly as if they had already been struck.

But he had gone too far to turn back now.

"Psych," he said, bland as Fred Astaire. "That's a nice major."

In a Fred Astaire world, the blond would have answered him, and Cyril would have danced her away.

Instead, he found himself staring into Rod's angry face.

Ooops, Cyril said to himself.

8

"What are you cutters doing here?" Rod said. "Did you get lost?"

"No," Mike said blandly.

"Then why don't you get lost now?" Rod said.

A bunch of Rod's buddies laughed, as if he had just said the funniest thing in the world. They began to form a loose circle around the intruders.

Cyril sensed the inevitable. "Ooops," he said, "I feel like that cartoon again."

Cyril and Moocher looked at Mike. They wanted a sign from him, something that would tell them what to do.

Except that Mike didn't know what to do. He was on the spot. It wasn't that he was afraid of a fight, it was just that he was off his turf, in enemy territory.

Mike thought quickly. "Is that him, Cyril?"

Cyril caught on immediately. "I don't think so," he said.

"Let's get out of here," Moocher said, almost before Cyril had finished his sentence.

It would have been all over, with not much face lost on either side, but just then Rod said exactly the wrong thing.

He looked at Moocher and said, "Smart move, Shorty."

Moocher caught Rod a good one right in the food tray, spilling the drinks intended for the lovely throat of the blond freshman.

Rod fell back to get his balance, knocking a table down. His friends—about fifty of them, it looked like—jumped to his aid. The cutters were surrounded. The only escape route was into the cafeteria line.

Somebody hit Mike and he smacked into a service shelf, knocking down several rows of plates, saucers, and cups, which hit the floor with a satisfying crash.

Cyril started swinging the bowling ball around for protection. He was a whole wrecking crew all by himself, and no one dared get inside the ball's arc. He wasn't being too careful where he pointed the thing, so he smashed a couple of rows of plates, which added to the image of random violence that he hoped would keep him from getting decked.

Rod and the other college guys formed a flying wedge and tried to advance, T formation style, but they had Cyril's deadly bowling ball to contend with, and Mike and Moocher were throwing whatever came to hand—chinaware, stray items of food, the occasional egg salad sandwich, Jell-O mold, or cold cut plate.

Rod's buddies were throwing back whatever they could find on their side. They didn't have the resources of the cafeteria line, and so made do with abandoned pieces of pie, half-eaten cheeseburgers, and the like.

It was getting pretty hairy when the inevitable happened. Cyril's bowling ball flew off his hand and caught a sophomore sociology major from Joliet, Illinois, square in the stomach, sending the poor boy skidding under a row of tables.

The threat of the Ultimate Weapon removed, Rod's buddies took heart and swarmed all over Cyril and the guys.

Around the corner, on the other side of the L, Dave and Katherine were alone, everyone else having got up to see what was going on. Eventually, they couldn't just sit looking into each other's eyes any more. It sounded like World War II out there. They got up to have a look.

Dave saw his friends surrounded and fighting back valiantly. He wanted to help them, but he couldn't, not with Katherine there. The resulting explanation would be too complicated.

"What's going on?" Katherine said, to no one in particular.

"Just some cutters making trouble," a girl said.

This remark made Dave mad, and unable

to control himself, he plowed into the fight, lashing out against the first strange face he saw.

Katherine grabbed Dave's arm and tried to pull him back. She didn't want this nice Italian she was growing very fond of to get hurt, and she couldn't understand why he wanted to get mixed up in a local squabble in the first place. Watching Dave fight only confused her more. She couldn't tell which side he was on.

She saw the campus police come through the door, led by Mike's brother, and she grabbed Dave by an arm and pulled him out of the fray. In English she thought he would understand, she said, "We go, now." He followed obediently.

The campus cops broke up the fight pretty quick. They only had to brandish their billies, because everybody on both sides had heard about police brutality and Kent State, and while the college kids and cutters were perfectly willing to be on either the giving or receiving end of a Jell-O mold, they didn't want to get their skulls cracked.

Mike's brother had Rod in a regulation choke hold and was pulling him off of somebody —not even Rod could have said who, at this point. He looked angrily at Mike, sure that his brother had been responsible for this whole thing, whatever it was.

"The cutters started it," Rod said, as loud as he was able with his throat being choked.

This was the wrong thing to say to Mike's brother, who tightened his hold on Rod's throat.

• • •

Rod was wearing a tie and jacket, and it wasn't even Saturday night. It was early morning, in fact, and he and several other student "leaders" were standing in the office of the President of the university.

The President was standing behind his desk, speaking to the roomful of so-called campus leaders as if he were making a commencement speech.

Mike's brother was off in a corner of the room, trying to look as inconspicious as possible.

"Most of you," the President was saying, using a phrase that had served him well at many commencements, "will only spend four years here."

He resented having to make this speech. There always seemed to be something popping up in his life that prevented him from leading a graceful existence, presiding at lunches or having cocktails with potential donors.

"But to a lot of us," he went on, "Bloomington is our home, and I don't like the way you are behaving in my home. These needless hostilities have happened before. They will not happen again. If you feel compelled to compete with the kids from the town, then you will do it in a different arena."

He looked down at his desk, where many papers were spread out before him. "I am looking at a plan to open our intramural program to them. And as a starting point, in consultation with Mr. Armstrong, we have decided to expand the field of this year's Little 500 to include a team from the town."

He was talking about the college bike race

that had taken its name from the Formula-1 race at Indianapolis and had remained a sacrosanct preserve of the university and its students. A loud groan went up from the crowd.

"But, sir," Rod said, at his most sincere, "they're just not good enough. Having them in the race..."

Dave and Cyril were going along on their standard run near Dave's house. Dave was on his bike; Cyril was walking. Cyril was telling Dave about the fight because, as far as he knew, Dave hadn't been there.

"The funniest part," he was saying, "is that tough guy Mike didn't get a punch in. You should've been there."

Dave didn't want to keep talking. "I have to go," he said.

"Are you going to see Katherine?" Cyril asked.

"I . . . I have to go train," he said. "The Italians will be here soon. *Ciao*, Cyril."

He rode off before Cyril could question him further.

Moocher and Nancy were standing outside the courthouse. Nancy was wearing her best dress. She had fixed her hair up in the new way she had showed Moocher. Moocher was in one of his dark T-shirts. He was fishing through his pockets for money he knew he didn't have.

"I'll pay for it," Nancy said.

"What do you mean?" Moocher said, still fishing around. "I've got money."

"We can go Dutch," Nancy said.

"On a marriage license?" Moocher said indignantly.

They fell into silence.

"You know what?" Nancy said.

Moocher was lost in thought and didn't respond immediately. "What?" he asked finally.

"I'm scared," Nancy said, giggling. "But I like it," she added.

Dave, riding by, on the way to see Katherine, saw Moocher and Nancy going into the courthouse together. He wondered what they were doing there.

He was late for his date. He had spent too much time talking to Cyril. Cyril was a good guy, and a help, and God knows Cyril had put himself on the line for him, but if you weren't careful you could spend your life talking to guys like Cyril, and grow old and die.

Dave was thinking about all this when he found himself racing toward a light that had just turned yellow. Normally, he would have been supercautious, but now Enrico Gimondi was late, and nothing if not a daredevil, so he sped with wild abandon through the yellow light, just as it turned red. Let the peasants of Bloomington look out for him for a change, he thought to himself, instead of the other way around.

At that moment, one of the peasants had to stomp on his car brakes to avoid hitting the bike. The car's brakes were old, and the driver had to jump on them as if he were an aerialist coming down on a pail of water from a height of fifty feet. The other people in the car braced themselves to avoid getting slammed through the windshield.

Which was okay—Gimondi liked to keep the peasants on their toes—except that the peasant who had to stomp on his brakes was Dave's father, and the gentleman who was, along with his wife and children, in the car with Dave's father was a man who had expressed interest in purchasing the car that Mr. Stohler had just stalled, on account of having had to slam on the brakes so quick and hard.

But all Dave saw was his father out for a ride with customers. He waved and rode on.

Mr. Stohler had thought he had a sale in his pocket and now he was trying desperately to salvage it.

He turned the key, and the old clunker gasped, turning over a hair too slow, and then died out again.

So Mr. Stohler said, "You know what? I put premium gas in this baby by mistake. It hates expensive gas."

He laughed at his own joke and waited for the answering laugh from the family in the back. It never came.

What finally came was the tow truck. Had it not come, the car Mr. Stohler had been trying to sell might still be sitting there in the middle of the road to this very day.

The car was towed off, its nose pointing up in the air. Mr. Stohler was draped over the wheel, exhausted, like a harpooned fish, while the gentleman in the back tried to stop his children's tears. "Will you please stop crying," the man kept saying. "The car didn't really die. It's just an expression."

Mr. Stohler wasn't so sure.

"I should have hit him when I had my chance," Mr. Stohler told his wife. "He'd be dead now. No more worries."

He was trying to drink a glass of milk but it was spilling.

"I'll talk to him, dear," Mrs. Stohler said, hoping thereby to gain their son a stay of execution for at least a few more days. "I'll tell him he'll either have to get a job or go to college."

"College!" Mr. Stohler said, another arrow having been plunged into his heart. "So he can thumb his diploma at me."

Dave was upstairs in his room, lying on his bed, utterly exhausted, but unable to go to sleep. He could hear his parents talking downstairs.

"Dave's never thumbed anything at anybody," he heard his mother say.

His father had an answer for that, too. "That's because he hasn't been to college," his father said. "Besides, he's probably too stupid to get in."

"Don't say that," he heard his mother say. "He'll hear you."

"I don't care," he heard his enraged father say. "It's my house. He doesn't understand English, anyway."

Mrs. Stohler tried to steer the conversation in a different direction. "I'm sure he'll find a job somewhere," she said.

"He couldn't get a job to save his life," Mr. Stohler said. "He's worthless, Evelyn. I could die of shame every time I see him, lazy freeloader."

Dave rolled over on his bed and thought about what his father had said about him, and thought about his father's life, and wondered if his father was right.

9

"I discovered this place," Rod said. "Wait till you see it."

He had brought his Little 500 teammates out to the quarries, and was now making a big deal out of it, like the quarries were King Tut's tomb or something. His teammates had all brought their girls. Rod's girl was with him, too —Kath. After that day when the cutters had started up in the Union and Kath had seen him with that freshman, she had been a lot easier to get along with.

So now they were all out for the afternoon, taking a look around the old quarries, their talk and laughter reverberating off the stone.

They were like rich American tourists, not caring whether or not they disturbed the natives.

On the other side of the quarry, out of view, Mike and the guys were sitting on the rocks, staring into the water. In contrast to the college kids, their mood was subdued. There was a distance between them all now, both physical and emotional. Something had gone wrong.

The immediate problem was that Dave had said he didn't want to race in the Little 500.

As soon as the President of the university had made the announcement, Mike thought he had a foolproof way to show up those college guys once and for all, and on their own turf.

Of course, the whole plan revolved around Dave, who, with all that crazy training he had been doing, was the closest thing to a pro Mike had ever seen. Without Dave, there simply wasn't a team. Anybody knew that.

And now here was Dave, saying he didn't want to race.

"And why not?" Mike asked. He was dangerously close to rage. He had come up with the foolproof plan and he wasn't going to let Dave take it away from him without a fight.

"I just . . ." Dave hesitated, "I just, uh, don't want to be in the Little 500."

"I thought you'd jump at the chance," Mike said.

"Well," Dave started to say, "I just . . ." He paused, and looked over at Cyril, who knew very well why Dave didn't want to be in the race. "I just don't want to be seen with all those college kids," he finished lamely.

"That's the whole point," Mike said, excitedly. "They'll all be there. We can beat those jerks in front of everybody."

"It takes four guys to have a team," Moocher said.

"We got four," Mike snapped. He was angry at Moocher for being too stupid to figure out the scheme. "We all enter, just to get in, and Dave rides the whole thing, and we win."

"Sure," Dave said, pleased to be thought that good. "It's just that, uh," he groped around for something to say, "I'll be working that day."

"Working! Since when?" Mike couldn't have been more surprised.

"Yes," Dave said. "I'm getting a job." He was stuck with his story.

"By yourself," Mike said, accusing him.

"Yeah," Dave said, "I need the money."

Mike looked as if Dave had just turned him in to the cops. "Oh, that's just great," he said. "You're a real pal, Dave."

Moocher felt called upon to say something.

"Look," he said. "The time comes when we all . . ."

Mike didn't let him finish. "I wasn't talking to you," he snapped.

"I don't care," Moocher shot back. "You're not a quarterback here, you know."

Moocher had zapped Mike right in his most vulnerable spot, so Mike paid him back in kind. "At least I was once," he said. "Which is a lot better than being a midget all my life."

Moocher controlled his rage with difficulty. He just couldn't see himself hitting Mike.

Dave was upset to see his pals at each other's throats. "Hey, c'mon," he said.

Cyril was even more upset than Dave. He was starting to cry.

"Hey, *bambini*," Dave said. He couldn't take it any more. "*Che cosa*, eh?"

Mike went for the jugular. "Just drop that Italian stuff, eh?" he said. "I'm so sick of it."

Any camaraderie still remaining disappeared with that remark. A pall fell over the group. Moocher and Cyril looked over at Dave with sympathy. Nobody likes his fantasies blown sky high.

Mike was almost sorry for what he had said, but having gone this far, he felt compelled to continue enumerating his grievances.

"Driving you to bike races," he went on. "What am I, your private chauffeur, or something? I don't ever remember you paying for the gas. Sure, it's fun to win. Get all the glory for yourself. But when it comes time to do something for the rest of us, you back off. I think you're just afraid of those college guys."

"And you're not?" Moocher cut in.

"The only thing I'm afraid of," Mike said, slowly and distinctly, "is wasting the rest of my life with you guys."

Cyril was really crying now. "I thought that was the plan. We'd waste the rest of our lives together."

Mike stood up. He was going to leave. He was ready to break up the gang right then and there, drive on home by himself, and let these idiots find their way home as best they could.

Just then Rod and his buddies and their girls appeared on the other side of the quarry.

Dave saw them, too. That is, he saw Katherine, and instinctively leaned back behind a rock, where he hoped he wouldn't be seen.

Mike and Rod stared at each other across the quarry pool. Uh oh, Cyril thought to himself. Bad Day at Black Rock time.

Katherine pulled at Rod's arm, but he brushed her off. He had no intention of moving.

Mike could feel the eyes of the guys on his back. He had to do something. He gestured to Rod, then at the water. Come on in, the gesture said. Then he ran up to the top of the rock he was standing on, and dove into the water. Rod followed him in with a higher, cleaner dive.

Once in the water, the two of them swam toward each other.

"They're going to race," Cyril said.

"What's he doing?" Dave asked. "That guy..."

This was a kind of competition Dave didn't understand.

But Mike and Rod understood it very well. Rod was smiling that maddening, arrogant, rich Texas smile. Piece of cake, the smile said.

Mike took off toward one end of the quarry, swimming as fast as he could. Rod stayed in place treading water for a minute, letting Mike get ahead. Then he smiled up at his friends and took off after Mike.

Mike was splashing clumsily, with none of Rod's style—he was not, after all, the captain of a college swimming team—but he was going as hard as he could churning up the water pretty good.

But nowhere near as good as Rod, who was smooth, powerful, and stylish. Rod caught up to Mike halfway across the quarry. He'd been breast stroking, keeping his head up out of the water, but when he came next to Mike, he rolled

121

easily over onto his back, and started a lazy backstroke, just like Esther Williams, which enabled him to look back at Mike and smile mockingly. No contest, the smile said.

Dave was watching from behind his rock, feeling lousy for having to hide. But better that than have Katherine see him out here, a cutter with his cutter buddies.

Rod reached the far side of the quarry, executed a perfect turn, and waited there for Mike, leaning back against the rocks like an Aquacade star on a Rose Bowl float.

Mike reached the wall exhausted, turning with what seemed like the last of his strength, and started back the way he had come.

Rod was amused. He had thought the race was over. But the cutter was a game little guy. If he wanted to race some more, Rod would race him. He pushed off from the rock and took off after Mike, imitating Mike's clumsy style. Up on the rock, Rod's friends laughed appreciatively.

On the other side of the quarry, Mike's buddies watched their friend being whipped and humiliated.

Rod got back across the quarry way ahead of Mike. Again he waited, still smiling, as Mike continued churning up the water, just bulling ahead, plowing through.

Mike was so tired and intent on keeping going that he didn't even see the edge of the pool when he reached it. He plowed into it and blood began pouring out of a cut on his forehead, staining the water in the quarry. But he was too driven, or too tired, to notice. He pushed off and started back again, barely able to move his arms.

Even Rod was starting to feel bad.

Up on the rock, the guys were getting worried.

"How long is he going to keep going?" Moocher said.

"Not much longer," Cyril said. "There won't be any water left, the way he's splashing."

But it wasn't funny. Mike looked like he was half-drowning out there. He'd lost his sense of direction, he had his own blood in his eyes, and he couldn't see where he was going. He wasn't swimming in a straight line any more. He was doing strange zigzags, going from side to side like an exhausted waterbug. He kept bumping into the sides of the quarry, hitting the sides with his hands. His hands were bleeding now, too. But he kept on going, splashing pathetically and defiantly through the bloody water.

Rod was treading water in the middle of the quarry, not sure what to do. He couldn't understand why Mike kept churning away in that blind, crippled way. Didn't he know the race was over? Didn't he know he'd lost?

Finally, Rod got disgusted. There were some losers who were so dumb they didn't even know they had lost. Well, it wasn't up to Rod to straighten him out. You couldn't send a guy a telegram out in the middle of the water, especially if he couldn't see.

Rod swam over to the side and climbed out of the quarry, back up to where his adoring friends were waiting. He toweled off, put his clothes back on, and he and his friends got out of there.

From his hiding place behind the rock,

123

Dave watched Katherine leave with Rod. He was angry at her for being with him, almost as angry as he was at himself for hiding.

As soon as she was out of sight, he left his hiding place and jumped into the water.

Mike was still swimming around, in a total daze now, working entirely on reflex, with no idea of what he was doing or why. Blood kept dripping down his face, sliding off his chin into the water.

Dave swam toward him. Moocher and Cyril were both in the water now, too, backing Dave up, if it became necessary.

Somehow Mike knew that Dave was there. His arms went around Dave's neck. He was even smiling a little through the pain. Dave had come to get him. Somebody still cared.

As he relaxed, Mike let his weight lean against Dave, and the two of them went down below the water's surface for a moment, down where it was dark and peaceful and you could rest and not have to prove anything to anybody. It made you want to stay, and stop fighting.

Then they came back up.

10

Nancy was worried about Dave's dad.

She was working as a waitress at Nick's Bar and Grill, the job as head cashier not having worked out, and here was Mr. Stohler sitting at the bar, doing exactly what the doctor had told him not to do.

"One more," Mr. Stohler said. "And make it a double."

Nancy tried to reason with him. "Haven't you had enough, Mr. Stohler?"

Mr. Stohler got truculent, as so often happened when you told a person he'd had enough.

"I've had enough of your lip," he said, "that's for sure. I said I want a double, and I want a double 'on the double.'" Angry as he was, Mr. Stohler grinned at his own wit.

Nervously, Nancy looked over at Nick, the

owner of the place. Nick gave her a nod that said, do what the man says. But Nancy didn't know if she should take the responsibility. Instead of doing what Nick wanted, she picked up the phone and dialed.

In a moment, Mrs. Stohler came on the line.

"Mrs. Stohler," Nancy said. "This is Nancy, down at Nick's. I think you'd better come down."

Mrs. Stohler came rushing in through the door of Nick's bar, fear written all over her face. Her husband was still at the counter. Nancy gave her a look of relief.

Mrs. Stohler wasted no time with preliminaries. "How much did he have?" she asked Nancy.

Nancy thought for a moment, wanting to be accurate. "Well," she began, "he started off with a single order of french fries. Then he had some onion rings. And then he ordered a double order of each." She gestured at Mr. Stohler's plate. "Right now he's on a cheeseburger deluxe."

Mrs. Stohler paled. She rushed over to her husband.

"C'mon, dear," she coaxed him. "You've had enough."

Mr. Stohler's mouth was full of wonderful, greasy food. He spoke through the food. "Leave me alone," he mumbled.

"Oh," Mrs. Stohler said, as if she were speaking to a small child, "you've got catsup all over your shirt. C'mon. Let's go home."

Mr. and Mrs. Stohler walked through town together, Mr. Stohler belching in the only contentment he'd known for weeks. He was talking about what was bothering him. He was talking about Dave.

"I'm just tired of it, Evelyn," he said. "I'm tired of worrying about him. Who'd hire a guy like that? He'll wind up a bum." And then he added what bothered him most: "An *Italian* bum."

"You could use some help at the lot," Mrs. Stohler said. "What if you gave him a job?"

"I don't want him selling used cars," Mr. Stohler said. He still hoped against hope that his son would make more of himself than that.

"Why not?" his wife asked. "If it's good enough for you . . ."

"Who says it's good enough for me?" Mr. Stohler snapped.

"You do," she reminded him.

"Well, it is good enough for me," he said gruffly, back on the defensive again. "But . . . I don't need help. Besides, he'd ruin me if I hired him. A weirdo like that . . ."

He had visions of Dave talking to customers in Italian. He cringed and belched again.

Dave sat in his room, looking at the walls. They didn't hold the fascination for him they usually did, not in his present mood.

He flipped through his *Sports Illustrated* magazine. He looked at his favorite picture, the picture of the smiling team Cinzano, with their arms around each other. He read the caption for the hundredth time: TEAM CINZANO TO RACE INDIANAPOLIS.

He heard a car pull into the driveway and looked up. His parents were home. Setting his magazine down, he went downstairs. He wanted to talk to his father.

When his parents walked into the living room, Dave was waiting for them.

"I want to talk to you," his father said, without preamble.

"Yes, Papa," Dave said. "I want to talk to you, too."

"You know what you're going to do," Mr. Stohler said. It wasn't a question.

"I'm going to get a job," Dave said.

Mr. Stohler's mouth dropped open. Somehow, Dave had managed to take the play away from him again. He had come in here prepared to say to his son, "You're going to get a job," and now he felt cheated.

"You see," Mrs. Stohler said, beaming proudly at her son.

"I see nothing," Mr. Stohler snapped. He wasn't going to concede defeat that easily. Glowering at Dave, he said, "*Where* are you going to get a job?"

"This car wash place is still hiring," Dave said. He was thinking of the place where Moocher had assassinated the time clock.

"Car wash!" Mr. Stohler's voice was full of contempt. "Car wash! You should've died when you had the German measles. No son of mine is going to wash cars."

The next day, Dave was whistling one of Enrico Gimondi's happy Neapolitan songs and washing a car.

He was washing one of his father's cars.

128

He was on his father's car lot, working for his father, washing one of his father's used cars, no doubt because his mother had put pressure on his father. He was having a nice time. The light physical labor was relaxing. And he would have money. Money to go to Indianapolis. Money to take Katherina somewhere nice.

Mr. Stohler, arms folded over his gut, watched his son wash the car. Dave was whistling while he worked. The boy shouldn't be whistling, Mr. Stohler thought to himself. If you whistled, you were having a good time. Dave wasn't supposed to be having a good time, he was supposed to be working.

"Hey," Mr. Stohler said, when it got too much for him, "no whistling. You're a shag boy, so shag. If I wanted whistling, I'd get a bird."

Amiable as ever, Dave stopped whistling and kept on washing the car. He could see the sun reflected in the car's windows. It made him happy.

Late that evening, Dave was still washing cars. The neon sign that said CAMPUS CARS was now reflected in the windows. It glowed like rubies. Then it went out.

Mr. Stohler had shut it off.

"How're you feeling?" he asked Dave.

"Tired, Papa."

Mr. Stohler smiled his satisfaction. "Exhausted?"

"Yes."

"Good," Mr. Stohler said. "You might as well get used to it. From now on, it's more of the same. Let's go home."

"I have to train," Dave said.

Mr. Stohler was a little disappointed. He pictured himself and his son going home together after a hard day's work. But Dave was off riding his Italian bicycle, even at night.

The same routine continued for the next few days. Dave would work all day, and train at night. Every once in a while the guys would come by in Mike's car and wave at him. That was nice.

And once, a bunch of fraternity guys passed by on their bikes. They were all wearing Little 500 T-shirts, and Rod was leading them. That was not so nice.

On days when it rained, there wasn't much to do. You couldn't wash cars in the rain. On those days, Dave would set up his bike in its stationary position and get in a little training. All the time he trained, he would think of the Italian team, their arms around each other smiling for their fans. Sometimes Dave saw himself in the middle, his arms around his teammates, smiling just like them. Once while pedaling he closed his eyes to savor the image and lost his balance and fell off his bike onto the ground. The Italian music in his head came to a stop.

Dave was really pushing himself too hard, and Katherine noticed. One night, when they were having coffee, she asked him, "Are you all right?"

"Sì . . ." he told her, pleased at her concern. "I just study too hard. I have big exam tomorrow."

"Are you going back to Italy in the summer?" she asked.

"Sì," he said. "My papa needs help."

Katherine's face broke into one of those smiles Dave was so crazy about. "Well," she said, sounding like someone who had a terrific secret and was just bursting to tell it, "I called up my parents. I'm getting a graduation present."

Dave looked up with more attention. He hadn't known she was that much older than he. He had assumed she was a couple of years younger than Rod.

"We can go to Italy together," she said, with that wonderful smile.

Enrico Gimondi almost choked on his coffee.

"Maybe I have to go to summer school," he said finally.

Katherine felt hurt. She couldn't understand why he didn't seem pleased at her news.

The following day, Dave asked his father, "Papa, can I have this Saturday off?"

"Of course not," Mr. Stohler said. He didn't even stop to think about it.

"Just this once," Dave pleaded. He was talking about what was, aside from Katherine, the most important thing in his life. "You see, the Italians are coming Saturday."

If he'd stopped to think about it, Dave would have realized this was not the way to get to his father.

"I don't care if the who's coming," Mr. Stohler said.

Dave was crushed. The idea of missing the team Cinzano was unthinkable.

"But I've waited so long," he said.

"No," Mr. Stohler said again. "N-double-O-NO-O." And then he repeated himself: "No." But he meant something else. He had just seen something. And he didn't like what he saw.

HOMECOMING QUEEN was coming home.

And not under her own power.

A bunch of college kids, including the blond guy who had bought it, were pushing the little sports car onto the lot.

"You stay out of this," Mr. Stohler said to Dave.

A few minutes later, Mr. Stohler was leaning all his weight against the hood of HOMECOMING QUEEN, pushing as hard as he could. What he was trying to do was get HOMECOMING QUEEN off his lot and back out on the street where it belonged. This was not proving very easy to do, mostly because the college kid who had bought the zippy little number, and several of his friends, were at the rear of HOMECOMING QUEEN, pushing as hard as they could in the other direction.

"What guarantee?" Mr. Stohler was saying, puffing very hard.

"You gave me your word," the blond college kid yelled.

"On paper?" Mr. Stohler yelled back, puffing as he did. "Can I see it on paper?"

The college kid was puffing a little, too, but nowhere near as hard as Mr. Stohler. "There was no paper," he said. "You gave me your word."

"I don't remember giving my word," Mr.

Stohler said, giving HOMECOMING QUEEN an extra hard push. "Now get this car out of here."

His son appeared at his side. Mr. Stohler had a sudden sinking feeling.

"You did, Papa," his son said. "You gave him your word. I heard you. We are poor, but we're honest."

Mr. Stohler was stunned. Insanity was one thing, but patricide was something else again. There was only one answer. This was not his son. It looked like his son, and indeed had been his son at one time, but the poor lad was insane now and could not be considered his son by any stretch of the imagination. He did not know the person who had just said what this boy had said. And in an Italian accent, at that. It would be easy to convince these college kids that he didn't know who this crazy Italian was. So he acted accordingly.

"What?" he said, and the startled tone in his voice was no act. "Who're you?"

Then he started to push on the hood of HOMECOMING QUEEN again, harder than he had ever pushed in his life.

"All I want is a refund," the blond college kid persisted.

Now the kid had done it. Perhaps the only thing in the world more dangerous than using a word connoting lack of stature to Moocher was to pronounce the word "refund" in the presence of Mr. Stohler.

Mr. Stohler repeated the blasphemous word aloud to himself, as if to make sure he'd heard it correctly.

"Refund," he said, hating the sound of the

syllables as they passed through his lips. He said it again, louder: "REFUND!"

He pushed even harder. "Are you crazy?" he asked the college kid, rhetorically. And then he repeated the word again, "Refund!"

He was getting very red in the face. He was pushing for all he was worth. Sisyphus, pushing that rock up that hill only to have it come sliding back down again, never pushed harder or more futilely than Mr. Stohler pushed HOMECOMING QUEEN. And all the while, the college kid and his buddies were pushing hard the other way.

Dave, whom Mr. Stohler had mentally disowned, made no move to come to his father's assistance.

It was just about then that Mr. Stohler became a fanatic, crossing the border between determination and madness. His whole life became centered on one goal: pushing the car off his lot and out of his life. The veins swelled in his neck, standing out like ropes. Blood rushed to his head, and his vision started to blur. Still, he kept on pushing. He had no choice.

"Re-fund," he kept saying, "refund." It had become a chant, an incantation. He said it in rhythm with his pushing. He understood the meaning of the word for the first time in his life, understood its derivation, broke it down into its component parts: Return the Funds, is what it meant, and Mr. Stohler was not about to do that, not if it was the last thing he did.

It very nearly was.

Everything around him started spinning. He couldn't see a thing. He had no balance. A huge pain stabbed his chest and spread up his arm. He clutched himself and started to fall backward. But with one last supreme effort of will, he righted himself and managed to pitch forward onto the hood of HOMECOMING QUEEN.

Mr. Stohler regained consciousness to find a stethoscope pressed against his chest. He was still groggy. He kept muttering to himself the last word he remembered. "Refund. Refund." Then he added an extra syllable, so that what he was actually muttering was, "No refund. No refund." The thought absorbed him, and kept him alive. He didn't even feel the needle slide into his vein.

Dave and his mother were sitting at the kitchen table waiting for the doctor to come out of the bedroom. When he did, they stood up involuntarily, as if showing respect would make everything come out all right.

"Well," the doctor said, "it's not a stroke, and he won't croak, as we say." He chuckled at his own witticism and lit a cigarette.

"Seriously, Evelyn," he said, like a night-club comic going into the sentimental close of his act, "he's in terrible shape. He's a Mack truck with a Rabbit engine. Once he's up on his feet, he'd better start using them. Walking, exercising . . . something. Otherwise," he got jocular again, "it's taps city for him."

The doctor saw that his audience was not as amused as they might be. "Well, I got to go," he said, and headed out of the house.

Dave stared guiltily at his mother across the kitchen table.

"I ruined everything," he said.

She smiled sweetly at him, and he had the sudden, surprising thought that a long time ago, back before he was born, her smile might have been like Katherine's.

"No, you didn't," she said. "He needed a rest, and now he's getting one."

Dave was moved to make the supreme sacrifice.

"I don't think I'll go to the race," he said. "I should be here when Papa wakes up."

She gave him the smile again.

"No," she said, "I don't think you should."

She reached into her purse.

"Here," she said. "Did I ever show you this?"

She pulled a document in a small green folder out of her purse and put it on the table.

Dave immediately recognized it for what it was.

"It's a passport," he said.

His mother nodded, and smiled at him again.

"They're really quite cheap, you know. A real bargain. I always carry it with me. One of these days there'll be a new girl at the IGA and when I want to cash a check she'll ask me for some identification and I'll take out my passport, and I'll say, 'Here.'" She paused and smiled again. "Won't that be something."

Dave found himself very moved to learn that his mother had been keeping a passport all this time. He understood the yearning it implied. He also knew that the passport was probably never going to be stamped.

His mother wasn't going anywhere.

"Oh, Mama," he said tenderly, and put his hand over hers.

But Mrs. Stohler didn't want his sympathy.

"So," she said, as if it were already settled. "I think you should go. I think you should come home singing, with a trophy." She sighed a little, for all the songs she hadn't sung, and the trophies she hadn't brought home. "You should do all that while you can," she said.

Dave was very moved. "I win this one for you, Mama," he said, and threw his arms around her.

"Now that would be nice," Mrs. Stohler said.

11

The day of the race dawned clear and bright.

For a long time, Dave had been afraid the day would never come. But it had, and now he was thinking how exciting it was to be going to Indianapolis, where the team Cinzano would be racing.

Mike drove him over, with Dave's bike on top of the car, just as if they had never had an argument. Just as if the guys had never broken up. They all decided, without saying it, that that day out at the quarry was best forgotten.

It seemed like they would never get there. Dave was like a little kid, looking out the car window at the mileage signs, wanting the trip to be over, wanting to *be there*.

The team Cinzano was posing for pictures,

looking just like their publicity photos. Just like in *Sports Illustrated*. Sleek and elegant, dressed in black, they looked rather sinister as they smiled and waved, striking very precise poses, making sure their hands and arms didn't obscure the name CINZANO on their jerseys.

The announcer was out on the track, telling the people what they were going to see.

"We are proud to have with us today the famous team Cinzano from Italy," he intoned. "They are touring America and so far are undefeated. Later on they have been kind enough to agree to hold a racing clinic which none of you should miss."

Dave was in the crowd of other racers, and like all of them, his eyes were glued to the Italians. He couldn't stop looking at them.

"Everybody please move to the starting line," the announcer said.

Dave put a banana and an apple in the back pocket of his jersey. Everyone seemed to be doing the same thing, stocking up on bananas.

From his position in the middle of a large pack, he looked over to the sidelines, where he could see Mike, Moocher, and Cyril. He waved at them.

The team Cinzano was at the front of the pack. Leaders of the pack, Dave thought. They looked very businesslike, and stared straight ahead.

The announcer's voice wafted across the field: "Riders ready! Timers ready!"

Dave felt a surge of excitement in his belly. In a minute, the gun would go off, and he would be racing against the team Cinzano themselves. Maybe he would be outclassed, but at least he would have done it. And he would give it his best.

The gun fired. The Italians took off, breaking beautifully, immediately separating themselves from the pack.

Behind them, the huge pack of riders started to separate into its various parts, like an amoeba reproducing itself. Already, there were stragglers. Several riders dropped back immediately, out of contention, realizing, whether they wanted to or not, that they were on a track that was far too fast for them.

Soon the riders were out in open country. The Italians, of course, were well out in front. Only about half a dozen other riders were able to keep up with them. Dave was one of them.

The rest were about half a mile back. Some of the riders were already eating their bananas. Others were drinking water.

The Italians approached a hill. Without any discernible signal being passed, they all shifted gears at the same instant and started sprinting up the hill.

Behind them, taking their cue from the Italians, the other front runners did the same, in hot pursuit of the Italians. Strain showed on the face of everyone, including the Italians.

From a distance, the riders looked like ants, steadily climbing up a steep hill.

The Italians appeared at the crest of the hill. They looked back over their shoulders and saw nobody behind them. They were way out in front again, as they were accustomed to being, and no challengers seemed to be in the offing. They were going to win at Indianapolis as easily as they had won everywhere else in this country.

Nodding to each other, relaxing a bit now, they shifted into high gear for the descent.

Dave appeared at the crest of the hill a moment or so later, with three other riders only slightly behind. As he started his descent, he shifted gears and poured it on, starting to sprint, leaving the other riders behind. Try as they might, they couldn't match him. He was just too good.

Coming down the hill, the Italians bent over their frames in the classic descent position, knees and elbows tucked in. They were coasting. They had it made.

Behind them, Dave raced down the hill, bent forward in a similar position. He was pumping away as hard as he could. He was deadly serious. He had begun to entertain a most amazing thought. It astonished him, but he went along with it.

He thought maybe he could beat the Italians.

For their part, the Italians were still coasting down the hill in perfect descent position. The hill was very steep, so even though they were coasting, they were going quite fast. One of them took a look behind him, to see if any of the Americans was anywhere around.

He saw Dave, bent over, breathing hard, pumping away like crazy.

When Dave realized that a member of the team Cinzano was looking at him, he looked up and smiled, and called out as if he were out for a pleasant afternoon stroll, *"Buon giorno. Come sta?"*

The Italians were stunned. They didn't know what was going on. American riders weren't supposed to keep up with them. They weren't supposed to talk in the middle of races. Most especially, these riders weren't supposed to talk *Italian* to them in the middle of races. The Italian in the lead was particularly annoyed. The one holding up the rear, closest to Dave, seemed amused. This kid was game, his smile seemed to say.

The Italians were riding hard now, something they hadn't thought they would have to do. They looked tired.

Dave was still behind them. He was tired, too. But when the lead Italian looked back to see how Dave was doing, Dave managed to smile again. It cost him a lot, but he did it.

This seemed to infuriate the lead Italian who gestured angrily to Dave, to move on up and take the lead, out on the point.

Dave was thrilled. He was so moved by the gesture that he failed to discern the anger in it. All he knew was that the lead racer of the legendary team Cinzano had gestured to him, to *Dave Stohler*, to take the lead. Which Dave did, with an extra burst of strength, pausing to pass a pleasantry to the lead Italian as he did so:

"*Oggi fa caldo, non è vero?*" Which was straight out of the Italian phrase book and meant, "It's hot today, isn't it?"

"*Roba da chiodi!*" the lead racer replied, and meant, "You don't say!" and could not possibly have been construed as a friendly remark.

Dave was out in front now, helping his adversaries, breaking the wind for them, letting

143

them come in behind him on his slipstream, as he had done with the truck that bore the same name the Italians carried so proudly on their chests.

It was proud work, but it was hard work, too, and he was getting tired. So were the Italians behind him. He could tell that. He knew they were pros; they were, after all, the team Cinzano, so when he began to lose wind and falter, he swung aside to let a member of the team get back out in front of him.

The lead member of the team Cinzano pulled out in front.

As the lead Italian passed him, Dave summoned up another conversational gambit out of the Italian phrase book: *"Che tempo fara piovera?"* Which translates as, "Do you think it'll rain?" and is, in any language, what you say when you have no real question to ask and are only trying to be pleasant.

"Filare!" said the lead Italian, on his way past Dave. This translates variously as "Scram!" or, "Get out of here," and was definitely not in the same friendly spirit as Dave's remark.

The Italian bringing up the rear tried to calm his buddy down.

"Not te la prendere!" he shouted, which translates as "Don't get your self worked up." The last Italian liked Dave's spirit, and wanted to keep this thing friendly.

But the leader rider wanted to get rid of Dave, once and for all, and coast on in to victory, as was his custom.

As they began the ascent up the next hill, the Italians switched off again. Once more, it was Dave's turn to take the lead. He was still holding his own with them, and that didn't make the Italians any too happy.

As Dave moved forward into position, the lead Italian reached over and shoved Dave's gear shift lever all the way forward, moving him into a very high gear. Dave had to pump so hard to make one revolution, he could hardly manage it.

"Mi scusi!" the Italian said, smiling, and took off, his teammates following, while Dave fumbled around, trying to get back into the right gear, wondering, as he did, if this was how the team Cinzano went around the world winning all its races.

> *No rider shall touch another rider. In case of such behavior, disqualification may result at the discretion of the Referee. When two riders come in contact or collision to the injury of the chance of either, it shall lie with the Referee to determine the one at fault.*

There was no Referee, of course, not out on the back roads. There was nothing for Dave to do but get mad, and hope to get even.

A few minutes later, riding as hard as he ever had in his life, Dave whizzed past the Italian team and took the lead again. He was playing for keeps now. Leading the way, he saw a huge pothole in front of him, untouched by the State Road Commission. He rode right toward the pothole and swerved sharply at the last minute. Behind him, the lead Italian rode right into the pothole, jarring himself badly.

Dave looked back and smiled into the angry Italian's face.

145

"Mi scusi!" he said.

The rear Italian seemed to appreciate the little reversal, but the one in the lead got a brutal look on his face. He was going to take care of this American twerp and this time he would make sure.

They were down on the flats now, just Dave and the four members of the team Cinzano. Everyone else had been left far behind.

The five of them were taking turns being in the lead. They approached a small hill. A while back, it would have seemed like a small hill. Now, it loomed like Everest. The lead Italian pointed at it. Dave was far too exhausted to fake a smile. It would take all his strength to pump his way up. His legs felt as if they would fall off and roll away if he foolishly tried to lift them one more time. Still, it was his turn, and he took it.

He tried to take his mind off what he was doing. He knew if he thought how tired he was, he would never make it. He tried to remember every name his father had ever given a used car.

Somehow, he reached the crest of the hill, out in front of the pack.

He was too exhausted to look back, and therefore he didn't see the second Italian, behind him, take his pump out of his emergency road kit. Dave swerved to the side to let the second Italian take the lead, as the practice of the last several minutes dictated.

But the first Italian pulled in behind him to block his way as Dave prepared to drop back. And the third Italian sprinted up ahead of Dave

146

and cut across in front, to block him if he should try to pull out that way.

He was caught in a squeeze play.

In front of him, the third Italian put on his brakes.

Dave put on his, to avoid running into the Italian's rear.

The second Italian, who was now beside Dave, reached across and stuck his pump into Dave's rear wheel.

Dave saw all of this in the split second it took to happen, but there was nothing he could do.

His wheel collapsed, his bike collapsed.

He wobbled off the road and tumbled down the steep grade, coming to rest at the bottom of a short hill on cool, green grass.

Up ahead, he could see the Italians ride off toward another win, still undefeated, their reputations intact.

He could hear the lead member of the team shout exuberantly to his buddies, and Dave didn't need a phrase book to figure out what was meant.

"Bravo! Bravo! Bella roba!"

Dave leaned back on the grass. His leg had been twisted in the fall, and it hurt him badly, but it wasn't broken. What had been broken, and what would not heal, were his dreams of glory, of sportsmanship, of being someone other than he was, of being special, of not being Dave Stohler, the cutter's kid.

The four members of the team Cinzano sprinted toward the finish line, easy, relaxed, plenty of wind left. A big cloth banner, FINISH, fluttered in the breeze.

The Italian who actually crossed the finish line first was the one who had been bringing up the rear, the one who had admired Dave's spunk. He did not approve of the way his team had won, and as he crossed the line, he turned and made a threatening gesture to his teammates.

Later, as the members of the team Cinzano were posing for their winners' pictures, the crowd around them cheering, Mike, Cyril, and Moocher had their eyes fixed on the track, waiting for Dave. They hadn't really expected him to win, but they had thought he'd do better. The race had been over for nearly twenty minutes, and he still hadn't shown up. Neither had any of the other local contestants, but that didn't mean anything. Dave was a lot better than they were.

From the 1978 Racing Rules, Constitution and Bylaws of the United States Cycling Federation, under the general heading PROTESTS:

Any objection regarding foul riding, starting off the wrong mark or such like offense committed during a race shall be made to the Referee immediately after the heat or race, and before the prizes are distributed. Failure to do this shall cause the party protesting to waive all rights to any prize.

All protests must be made in writing, signed by the objector, and accompanied by a deposit as specified in the Schedule of Fees. Such protests must be handed to the Referee who will take proper action upon it. Riders may supplement such action with additional information sent direct to the Board of Appeals.

In road races, all protests in regard to foul riding or other infraction of any of these rules must be presented to the Referee or his duly authorized representative in writing within one (1) hour after the finish of the race and must be accompanied by a deposit as specified in the Schedule of Fees.

There would be no protests today. An hour later, Dave was in the back seat of Mike's car, ready to leave. His battered bike was strapped down on top. Round and round in his head ran the music of the second movement of Mendelsohn's Italian Symphony. It had once been his favorite, it was what ran in his head when he was racing at his best, but now it was just an irritant.

Mike drove by the finish line. A man was taking down the big cloth FINISH sign, which was still fluttering in the wind.

Everyone else was gone. The Italians were gone. They were probably in a hotel suite, being toasted with champagne. They had kept up their winning streak, after all, and were still undefeated in America.

Cyril broke what was becoming a very grim silence.

"I feel like one of those dwarfs," he said. "You know, when they think Snow White's dead."

Mike turned to Dave and said, "So I guess you're a cutter again, like the rest of us."

Dave heard the tone of malicious satisfac-

149

tion in Mike's voice, but he didn't have the energy to respond to it.

"I guess," he said, looking straight ahead down the road toward Bloomington, where they all came from, where they all lived, and where they would probably all stay.

What he knew, but didn't tell them, was that there had been a fatality in the race that afternoon.

Enrico Gimondi was dead, killed by his countrymen, waylaid on a back road in Indiana.

When they got to Bloomington and pulled up in front of Moocher's house, Dave noticed a small sign tacked over the FOR SALE sign. SOLD, it said.

It just seemed like one more thing. The end of a perfect day.

12

Mr. Stohler, now sufficiently recovered to be allowed to sit at the kitchen table, was explaining something to his wife.

"No," he was saying, "I don't feel lucky to be alive. I feel lucky I'm not dead. There's a difference."

The front door opened, and Dave came limping in. Blood was still caked all along his left leg, and his racing jersey was torn and filthy.

"What happened to you?" Mr. Stohler asked.

"It's nothing," Dave said. "How're you feeling, Dad?"

Mr. Stohler's jaw dropped on hearing the word he had thought would never issue forth from his son's lips again.

"Dad," Mr. Stohler repeated. Yes, that was

the word all right. His son had called him Dad. Which was nice, which was a welcome return to the old ways, but was still not enough to excuse what had been preying on Mr. Stohler's mind since falling across the hood of HOME-COMING QUEEN.

"I'll tell you how I'm feeling," he said. "I've had nightmares all night that everybody I ever sold a car to is going to come in and ask for a refund. And you'll be there handing out the checks." Mr. Stohler pantomimed the awful act: "One for you, and one for you . . ."

"I'm sorry I gave him back his money," Dave said. "I really am." He limped further into the room. "Everybody cheats, Dad. I just didn't know."

Mr. Stohler was only slightly less surprised than if his wife had suddenly announced she was running off with Robert Redford. Oddly enough he didn't feel triumphant. He actually felt a little ashamed.

"Well," he said, "now you know. So, where's the trophy?"

Suddenly, Dave couldn't hold himself any more. He had been suppressing his rage all afternoon, all the way back from the race, because he couldn't let go in front of the guys, but now here he was, in his own home, with only his mother and father to see, and he burst into tears.

"Oh, Dad . . ." he moaned, and rushed forward to throw his arms around his father.

Mr. Stohler didn't know what to do. His arms were outstretched, as if to begin an embrace, but he seemed unable to complete the motion.

"What?" he said, finally. "What is this?"

Dave didn't answer. He just kept on crying.

"Look," Mr. Stohler said. "You don't have to be this miserable. A little is all I asked for."

And then he put his arms around his son.

"What're you crying for?" he asked. "You'd think you lost your wallet or something."

He patted Dave's hair lightly, as if it might be on fire.

"Talk to him, Evelyn," Mr. Stohler pleaded. He looked over at his wife, only to see that she was crying, too.

"And what're you doing?" he asked.

She just shook her head. She couldn't tell him that the unlikely show of affection between her husband and her son had moved her to tears.

Mr. Stohler looked at his wife more closely, unable to read what was on her mind, but then he saw the beginning of a smile start to make its way through her tears.

The floor of Dave's room was a scene of carnage. There were crumpled Italians all over the floor, in various attitudes of ruin and defeat. Some of them had been ripped to shreds. Others had gaping holes in their middles. Dave ripped the last Italian poster off his wall and crumpled it up.

The cat yowled.

"You hungry, Jake, is that it?" he said.

Mr. Stohler stood in the doorway of his son's room. He saw the ruined Italians on the floor. He heard the cat called by its proper name. He thought he knew what was going on.

"Dave," he said.

"Yes, Dad."

"Let's go for a ride," Mr. Stohler said.

They drove to the campus. Mr. Stohler parked the car in one of the lots, and motioned to Dave to get out. For a while, they walked in silence together, enjoying the pleasant evening, the peacefulness of the campus, dark and quiet, with no one around.

As they passed one of the classroom buildings, Mr. Stohler pulled out a cigarette and lit it. Then he spoke, for the first time since he and Dave had left the house.

"Just one," he said. "Don't tell Mother."

He looked at the big building they were passing. "You know, I do this every now and then. Come here at night, and . . ." He paused for a moment, and then said what he had been wanting to say ever since they had arrived. "I cut the stone for that building over there."

Dave smiled and said, "Yes, I know, Dad."

"I was one fine stonecutter," Mr. Stohler said. "Mike's Dad . . . Moocher's . . . Cyril's . . . we all were. Well, Cyril's dad . . ." he started to say something, but this was not the time to be small-minded. "Ah, never mind. The thing is . . ." And then he paused again, because this was hard for him to say. "I loved it. I was young, slim, and strong, and proud of my work . . . and the buildings went up . . . and when the buildings were finished . . . strangest thing happened. It . . . It was like the buildings were too good for us." He shook his head, still puzzled at the way things worked. "Nobody told us that. But we just felt uncomfortable. Even now. I'd like to be able to stroll through the campus and look at the limestone, but I feel out of place."

He walked on for a moment in silence, Dave beside him. For some reason, Dave didn't feel embarrassed. He felt good. Sad, but nice.

"I suppose you guys still go swimming in the quarries," his father said, after a while.

"Sure."

"So, all you get from my twenty years of work is the holes we left behind."

"I don't mind," Dave said.

"I didn't, either, when I was your age," Mr. Stohler said. "But . . ." and then, instead of going on with his thought, he brought up something else that was on his mind. "Uh . . . Cyril's dad says he took that college exam."

"Yeah, both of us did."

"So, how did you . . ." Mr. Stohler paused to alter his sentence. "How did both of you do?"

"Well, I think, uh, one of us did all right. But neither of us . . ." and then, taking his cue from his father, Dave said what was on *his* mind: "I won't go, Dad." His anger began to come out. "I'm not ashamed of being a cutter. I don't want you feeling bad."

"Don't do me any favors," Mr. Stohler said gruffly. And then he thought he saw what was going on. "What, you afraid?"

"Yeah," Dave said, "a little. And then there's the rest of the guys."

"Well," Mr. Stohler said, "you took the exam. You did all right, huh?"

"Yeah."

"Well, that's . . ." he searched for the right word, something not too sentimental: "That's good. Your mom . . ." and here he was completely unable to say what he meant, so he just cut his thought off with: "She's a fine woman."

They both smiled. Neither knew quite what to do next. They had been sitting on a bench near the huge classroom building, and Mr. Stohler got up and put out his cigarette. Dave got up, too. Mr. Stohler put his arm around his son, and they walked back to the car together.

One thing Dave had that a lot of guys his age didn't have was a phone in his room, his own phone, with its own number. It had helped a lot the many times he had had to call Kathy. Who knows what his father would have said if he'd heard Dave talking to a girl and pretending to be Enrico Gimondi.

But now Enrico Gimondi was dead, killed by a fall from his bike as a result of an Italian having stuck a bicycle pump through his rear wheel, and it was time to tell Kathy that. Dave knew it was going to be the hardest thing he had ever done in his life.

He took a deep breath and walked around the room a couple of times, psyching himself up for the call. Finally, when he couldn't delay any longer, he picked up the phone and dialed the number of Katherine's sorority.

In a moment, a girl's voice came on the line. A pledge, no doubt, saying, "Good evening, Chi Delta Delta Sorority, may I help you, please?"

"Yes," Dave said, "can I speak to Ka . . ." he stumbled over the name, "Kathy, please."

Just then the doorbell rang. Dave heard Moocher's voice in the kitchen: "They sold my house and Dave said I could stay here for a bit."

He'd forgotten all about Moocher. He couldn't talk to Kathy with Moocher hanging around, and Moocher was sure to head straight for his room. He was glad the pledge hadn't found Kathy yet.

Moocher entered his room, carrying his barbell set. Cyril followed, carrying Moocher's suitcase.

"Can I sleep over, too?" Cyril said.

"The university bought my dad's house," Moocher said.

From out in the hall came the sound of Mr. Stohler's voice: "There goes the neighborhood," he said.

Later that night, outside on the street, Mike sat in his car looking at the light in Dave's window. An unlit cigarette was in his mouth. He was thinking about whether or not to join the guys.

The guys, all three of them, were sleeping on the floor of Dave's room. Or were supposed to be sleeping. Actually, all three of them were awake, looking at the ceiling, thinking.

Cyril broke the silence: "Our year's almost up . . . and . . . well . . . if anybody's got plans that don't include me, that's all right." He paused for a moment, and said, "I've got plans myself that don't include me."

He thought that was pretty funny, so he tried to laugh, but it wouldn't come. He put one arm around Dave, the other around Moocher, and closed his eyes and tried to go to sleep.

It took him a long time.

The next day, walking along with Moocher, Dave decided to talk to him about Katherine.

"I tried calling her to tell her," he said, "but I . . . I just couldn't do it."

"When she sees you in the race she'll find out," Moocher said. This was the first open acknowledgment that Dave would be racing in the Little 500. After what had happened at Indianapolis, the guys had just assumed it. "Maybe if she really likes you, she won't care. You know Nancy and I . . ." Moocher began, switching over to his constant topic.

But Dave cut him off. He knew it was rude, but he just didn't want to hear about Nancy and Moocher just then.

Happy couples made him mad.

He finally decided to wait for Katherine outside one of her classes. He knew her schedule by now, what classes she had a free hour after.

He didn't look like Enrico Gimondi any more. He had let his hair go back to its original curly style; he no longer wanted to torture it into the sleek Italian look. He no longer wanted to dress like an Italian, either. He had his jeans on. He was going to go the whole way. He was going to tell her who he was, and take the consequences, whatever they might be.

At first, she didn't recognize him. Then she was stunned. You would have thought someone had just slapped her across her face.

"Oh, my," she said, when she recovered her composure. "What did you do to your hair?"

Her words stabbed him like knives.

He was sure she was lost to him. She didn't

want him, she wanted Gimondi, the suave Italian, with his aura of mystery, and his family in the old country.

To add to the pain, Dave had never seen her look lovelier. Maybe it was just that he knew he was going to lose her, but her beauty blinded him.

He didn't know what to say, how to begin. He fumbled: "I . . . well . . . I just . . ."

She rode over his hesitancy, certain of what was best. "I liked it better before. You look like everybody else now."

She put her hands in his hair and started to play with it, trying to get it back to its original shape, trying to change him back to Enrico Gimondi, the guy she had begun to make a commitment to. She was the girl everybody was after, and now he had done this. It wasn't right.

Dave had only one thing to say to her. "I *am* everybody else." As soon as he said it, he knew that it was exactly what he meant to say, but it was too dead on, too much on the button, and he had to amend it somehow. "I mean . . ."

She wasn't having any of it. She laughed, that wonderful laugh that broke his heart. "You look funny," she said.

He tried again to begin: "You see, Katherine. . . ."

"Katherina!" she amended.

"I feel terrible," Dave said. He said it in his flat Midwestern accent, and Katherine, who was nobody's fool, began to feel just a little nervous.

"You sound real funny tonight," she said. "*Che cosa, amico?*"

"My name is Dave Stohler," Dave Stohler said.

Once again Katherine recoiled, as if she had been slapped. She had the look of a very great lady who had just been offered an impertinence.

"What's that supposed to mean?" she said. He had thrown her a curve, and all she had now to pull her through were her breeding and beauty. Both of which were more than a match for Dave.

"Nothing," he said. He moved his foot around in the dirt. With one fierce, offended question, she had reduced him from the Great Gimondi, a role he had been prepared to abdicate anyway, to an Indiana cutter, which he was beginning to feel like more and more all the time.

"It's just a name," he said, and then, having said that, he blurted out the rest. "I made it all up. I was born in Bloomington. I went to Bloomington High. I was the treasurer of the Latin Club and head of the ushers for assembly programs. I..."

"Stop kidding around," Katherine said. She was finding it hard not to believe him, but she didn't want to. She had banked on this guy. He had been different.

Dave kept right on going. "I'm what you call a 'cutter,'" he said. "Only I'm not really a cutter, either, so I don't know what I am."

It was the most honest thing he had ever said to anybody, but Katherine was in no condition to understand. All she knew was that she had been lied to, that she had believed the lie, had banked on it, had acted on it, and, more than he knew, had planned her future on it.

She was sinking fast, but desperately trying not to show how vulnerable she was. She came on strong and tough. She wanted some answers.

"And Napoli," she said, ". . . and the big family . . ."

Dave just nodded. The nod said it all.

Katherine fought back her tears, and even in his misery Dave could notice how beautiful she looked.

Despite her pain, Katherine was in awe of what Dave had done to her. She had left more than one guy stewing in his own juices, singing his sad song, and now somebody had done it to her, had sneaked up on her blind side, where she was vulnerable, and even though she hated him, she admired the talent involved. He had drawn blood. Whoever he was, cutter or not, he had made her care. A considerable achievement. So she gave him his due.

"Well, it was a good act," she said. "You certainly fooled me."

"I just didn't know how else . . ." Dave began, and then faltered, agonized.

"Do you know what you are?" she said.

He told her the truth. "No, I haven't a clue."

"I'll tell you what you are," she said, but could not continue and began to cry.

"I'll tell you," she said, trying again. "You . . . you . . ." But she found she couldn't. She couldn't talk at all.

She turned on her heels and ran back inside the classroom. She thought of it as a sanctuary, inviolate, like a ladies' room. He was a townie. A cutter. He couldn't follow her.

And he didn't. He watched her go, wincing as the door slammed behind her.

He was still standing in the same place when a few minutes later Katherine came running back out again, her hair flying, her eyes furious, furious and still beautiful.

He thought for a second that she had changed her mind and was running back into his arms—like in the old movies he liked so much.

She ran right up to him and rapped him across the mouth.

He took her blow without complaint. He deserved it, after all.

Then she hit him one more time, harder, and ran back to the classroom.

13

A couple of days later, the guys came over with a bike for Dave.

An American bike, the official bicycle of the Little 500. It looked heavy and ungainly beside Dave's sleek Italian racer. It also looked stripped bare. It didn't have a thing on it. As the United States Cycling Federation says:

For all track or sprint races, only a bicycle with a single cog fixed wheel and without a hand, coaster, or other mechanical brake shall be used.

All machines with appliances giving undue advantage over the riders of bicycles accepted as track bicycles in common understanding and as defined above shall be excluded from all track or sprint races by the Referee of the meet.

Dave looked at the bicycle. He put his hands on the handlebars. He didn't like the feel of it. It wasn't his bike.

The guys were watching him, apprehensively.

"Can't I even add some toe-clips?" Dave asked finally.

"No," Mike said. "It's official issue. They said you can't add or change a thing."

"It's a piece of junk!" Dave said.

"But it's got a nice personality," Cyril said, "and it's had its rabies shots already."

"I don't think it looks so bad," Moocher said.

"That's because you don't have to ride it," Dave told him.

Moocher was getting a little weary of Dave's attitude. "You don't have to, either, Dave," he said. "We're not going to beg you."

"Plead, perhaps," Cyril cut in, "but beg . . . never. We have our pride."

"Forget it," Mike said. "At least we got invited. That's something. I'll take it back."

He started to walk the bike to his car.

"You actually seem relieved, Mike," Dave said.

Mike stopped in his tracks.

"You don't think we can win any more, do you," Dave continued.

Mike didn't answer.

"Why not?" Dave asked him.

"Well," Mike said, after a long time, "maybe they *are* better."

"I've never heard you say that before," Dave said.

"That's because I never felt it before."

164

"My dad would be proud of you," Cyril said. "Our family motto is: It can't be done."

Dave looked at his friends. Here they all were, himself included, talking themselves into another failure. Not this time, he said to himself.

Aloud, he said, "We'll see about that."

He walked over to Mike and took the bike from him. He started wheeling it toward the garage. Then he got on it and rode it the rest of the way into the garage.

The guys looked at each other. They were smiling.

In a moment, they heard sounds of machinery starting up coming from the garage.

Their smiles got broader.

Dave turned the garage into a workshop. They hadn't given him much of a bike, but he was going to turn it into a better one.

First, he dismantled it. He took off the wheels, took the bearings out, and checked the gear alignment. He removed the aluminum crank. Holding the saddle in his hand, he pushed down on it. It was very hard.

He took the saddle into the kitchen, put it into a large pan, poured olive oil over it, put the pan on a hot plate, turned on the hot plate, and covered the pan. His mother watched him in fond puzzlement.

He centered the front wheel on a truing stand, then using the rim gauge, he adjusted the spoke tension to make the rim perfectly straight. When he was finished, he spun the wheel. It spun dead true.

He did the same to the rear wheel, dishing it to the right to center it over the axle locknuts,

165

putting fresh grease on the ball bearings. When he was done, it spun like a top.

He took the saddle out of the pan of olive oil. It didn't smell good, but it felt like glove leather.

After he had cleaned and regreased the crankshaft, he put it back together, taking out the sideplay by adjusting the side cup. He spun the chainwheel assembly. It spun fine and fast.

He took the chain out of the kerosene bath it had been soaking in and oiled it carefully.

He checked the tires.

He took up the slack in the brake cable.

He disassembled and cleaned the hub, then put it back together.

He aligned the pedals.

The last thing he did was put on handlebar tape.

When he was finished, he was dirty and the bike was clean.

He smiled with satisfaction.

It still wasn't much of a bike, but it was a better bike than the one he'd been given.

The next afternoon, he took the thing out for a spin. He wanted to test it, to test himself, to see how he and the machine would get along. The feel of the bike was subtly different from his own, and at first his hands and feet did not adjust. He hoped he could reprogram himself sufficiently by the time of the race to do as well as he knew he could on his own bike.

Well, who cares about them. He'd show them anyway.

He tried a sprint, but mid-way he suddenly stopped pedaling and reached down and

166

grabbed his left leg. He was in pain. He took his foot off the pedal and shook his leg, trying to shake off the cramp. It wouldn't go away.

He'd ignore it.

He would beat them all, cramp or not, lousy bike or not.

A little later, when his leg felt better, he decided he wanted a hot dog. There was hardly anybody in downtown Bloomington. Which was fine with him. He wasn't looking for company, just for a hot dog.

Parking his bike, he sat down on a curb near the hot dog stand and proceeded to eat.

The spring semester was over, otherwise there'd have been college kids all over the place, polluting the air. This way, the place was deserted, and a guy could relax and enjoy his food.

He took a big bite out of his hot dog.

"Hello," Katherine said.

He was stunned to see her. He had thought she'd be gone by now, graduated.

"What're you doing here?" he said.

She shrugged. She didn't want to tell him that she had spotted him when she'd turned the corner at the end of the block, and had waited several minutes before deciding whether to talk to him.

They smiled tentatively at each other.

"Guess what?" Katherine said.

Now it was Dave's turn to shrug. "I don't know," he said.

"I got a job in Chicago."

"Moocher's dad's in Chicago," Dave said. "He's . . ." and then he realized she didn't know who Moocher was, and waved the remark away with his hand.

"And I'm going to Italy after all," Katherine said. "With my parents."

Dave almost made an Italian gesture, but stopped before it got under way.

"I wish . . ." he said, "I wish you a nice trip."

"You, too," she said. The beginnings of a smile played at the edges of her lovely mouth.

Dave was puzzled by her remark. "I'm not going anywhere," he said.

Her smile grew larger.

"I don't know about that," she said.

Then she turned and walked away, and he let her do it.

Moocher was sleeping over at Dave's, which meant he was eating over, too.

Mr. Stohler, Dave, and Moocher were seated around the dining room table. Mrs. Stohler was out at the stove. She had fixed a good, plain meat and potatoes dinner, and Moocher was really putting it away.

Mr. Stohler watched him. Then he looked at the half head of lettuce and crackers on the plate in front of him.

Life was unfair.

Mr. Stohler couldn't just sit there and watch Moocher putting it away and not say something. That was asking too much of a man.

So he leaned over toward Moocher and said, "If you eat so much, Moocher, how come you're so small?"

Moocher wasn't going to get mad. It was Dave's dad talking, after all, and he was staying in Dave's dad's house and eating Dave's dad's food.

"It's my metabolism, Mr. Stohler," he said. "I eat three times a day, but my metabolism eats five times a day."

Mr. Stohler wished that he had a metabolism like that, so he could sit there and put it away, too.

He decided to change the subject.

"Well," he said, "I go back to work tomorrow."

Dave looked disappointed.

"Aren't you going to come and see us race, Dad?"

Mrs. Stohler came in from the kitchen, bearing more food not intended for her husband.

"He's afraid he'll bring you bad luck if he comes," she said.

Mr. Stohler didn't like his wife saying that in front of Dave. He had told it to her in private. He tried to cover it up.

"I've got work to do," he said gruffly, "that's all."

Then Mr. Stohler decided that as long as his wife was telling secrets, he would, too.

"Besides," he said, "there might be another metabolism to feed around here."

Dave dropped his fork.

"You mean you might be a father?" he said.

"Yes, I might," Mr. Stohler said, "and your mom might be a mother and you might be a brother." He was vastly pleased with himself. "That way," he finished, "I keep it all in the family."

Dave's head was spinning too fast for him to say anything.

His mother would be so happy. He would not be an only child any more. He was used to being an only child. He never had to share anything. But he was grown up now, or almost, and it might be nice to have a baby brother or sister to look after. Which would he rather have?

If it was a baby brother, he could teach him some of the stuff he knew, like racing, and show him how to avoid some of the mistakes he'd made.

If it was a baby sister, maybe she'd grow up to be as sweet and lovely and wise as Katherine, and guys would be after her all the time, and come on to her, and pretend to be things they weren't, as he had done, and maybe he'd have to punch them out.

Dave looked at his father. Then he looked at his mother. She was smiling at him. He looked back at his father again.

Then he couldn't contain himself any more. He jumped up and threw his arms around his mother.

"You must be very happy, Mr. Stohler," Moocher said.

"Of course I must," Mr. Stohler said. "You think I have any choice?"

Mrs. Stohler, still in her son's arms, called over to her husband, "You said you were going to give them a pep talk."

"They don't need pep, I need pep. Go ahead," he told his wife. "Give it to them."

Mrs. Stohler went out into the kitchen and opened up a drawer. She returned with some folded T-shirts in her hand. Moocher raised his eyebrows and looked over at Dave.

"We thought . . ." she began. She sounded as if about to make a presentation speech.

Her husband interrupted her. "Since you're going to be out there," he told the boys, "you might as well tell them who you are."

He looked at his son.

Dave got up from the table and took the T-shirts from his mother. He set them down on the table and picked up one of them and unfolded it.

On the back, in very large bold type, was printed:

CUTTERS.

Dave thought he was going to cry. But he wasn't quite sure why.

14

*A race of the type of the Little 500 is gen-
erally called a Madison, from the old six day
bicycle races in Madison Square Garden. It
is a relay race, in which one member of a
team may relieve his teammate at either's
discretion. When one member of a team gets
out far ahead of the field, he is said to be
breaking away.*

It was a good, clear day for the race. There
was a considerable turnout. With so many different teams out there, and each of the team
members having so many friends, a crowd was
assured. The crowd filled the grandstand, dressed
in the kind of colorful, improvised ensembles
that you used to see only at sporting events but
now see everywhere.

As the various teams entered the stadium

to take their places in their designated pit areas, they waved to their friends in the crowd. They looked brave and proud, like gladiators. One of the local high school bands recruited for the occasion was playing a triumphal march, adding a certain grandeur to the occasion.

Then the guys entered the arena, Dave pushing his bike along.

The first thing you noticed about them was their size. All of the other teams, having a choice of candidates, had picked members of as nearly the same height as possible, as they would be riding the same bicycle, with a set saddle position, and therefore the same leg length from seat to pedals.

Not the Cutters. Seen from the back, with their T-shirts announcing their name, they looked like this:

<blockquote>
CUTTERS
CUTTERS   CUTTERS
             CUTTERS
</blockquote>

They didn't even walk in step, like the other teams. They were all strung out, in a straggly line.

And they were nervous and jerky, like actors in a silent movie. Everything made them nervous. The crowd was roaring, and that made them nervous. The other teams looked very cool and self-contained, and that made them nervous.

But what made them most nervous was walking past the pit stop where Rod and his fraternity brothers were standing. Rod smiled that Texas smile of his and stared hard at Mike.

Mike couldn't look back and turned his head away. But not Cyril. Cyril looked right at

Rod, even smiled slightly, because Cyril felt safe in thinking that Rod and his buddies weren't going to rush out on the field and jump him in front of all these people.

It was time for the race to begin. The crowd was hushed. The Starter, an elegant-looking gentleman in a blue suit, called out from the track, in a voice that seemed to carry for miles, "Gentlemen, mount your bicycles!"

A great roar went up from the crowd.

A pace car, an open convertible, led the field around the track for one lap. Dignitaries from the campus sat in the open car, like politicians at a parade.

Then the pace car started to go faster, and the riders pedaled to keep up.

As the pace car completed its lap, the Starter waved his flag, and the pace car swerved off the track.

The race was on.

Right at the start, there was a mad scramble for position. Riders stretched out across the entire width of the field. Rod had taken an early lead.

Dave was dead last, but trying to move up.

His hair was now its natural curly self, and his T-shirt said CUTTER on the back. He looked like what he was, a young American kid on a bike.

He was riding brilliantly, always looking for openings, the way a superb race driver will in a crowded field, or a good everyday driver on a crowded freeway. Whenever a space revealed itself in the pattern of people ahead of him, he shot through it and moved up, and as

175

all the other riders went wide on the first turn, Dave took it on the inside, moving up three or four positions. It was a great intuitive move.

Even the three guys in Pit Area No. 34 could tell that it was a great move. They were jumping up and down and pounding on each other in their excitement.

"He's moving up," Cyril shouted. "Look at him go!"

The race was two hundred laps, on a quarter-mile track, four laps to the mile, a fifty-mile race. Dave knew he could do the whole fifty miles himself, if it came to that. He had done it before, the day he beat the Cinzano truck. As he completed the first lap, he looked up at the lap chart, a big board at one end of the field. A man's hand reached out and flipped the board; 199, it now said.

Mr. Stohler, dressed in tie, jacket, and hat, sat in a car in his parking lot. The motor was running, but the car wasn't moving. Mr. Stohler was listening to the broadcast of the race on his car radio.

He was well prepared for a long vigil. He had a large Noble Roman paper bag in his hand, stuffed with french fries and pizza.

On the car radio, the announcer said, "And so, after twenty-five laps, the perennial favorites are up front. Sigma Nu, Phi Kappa Psi, Sigma Alpha Epsilon . . . and here comes . . ." the announcer sounded puzzled and excited at the same time. "It's the Cutters!"

Mr. Stohler banged on the car horn a

couple of times and shoved a triangular wedge topped with sausage and onion into his mouth.

Dave was now within striking distance of the leaders. There was a black rider just behind him. Dave and the black rider caught up with the leaders, and now there were five teams out in front.

As the five lead riders swung around to the pit areas, the three riders from fraternity teams pulled off for an exchange. Entering their pit area, they slammed on their brakes, jumping off while the bike was still moving, allowing a fresh rider to jump on a moving bike.

Dave and the black rider didn't get replacements. Dave stayed in the lead for a while, but then the fresh riders caught up with him.

Rod sat in his pit area, resting. He was breathing hard. "He won't last," he said to his teammates. He didn't have to say who he was talking about.

Over in Pit Area No. 34, Mike kept saying, "He'll last. Won't he? He'll last."

"Stop saying 'last'" Cyril said, wincing.

Katherine sat in the stands, lovely in a lavender blouse and white shorts that showed off her legs. She hadn't intended to come. She told herself she had just wandered by. Now she found herself caught up in Dave's performance, getting excited. She hadn't intended to do that, either.

Dave was beginning to hurt. His left leg was starting to bother him, the one that had got the cramp. He tried not to think about it. As he went around a turn, his left foot slipped

177

off the pedal. For a moment, it was pretty hairy; he almost lost his balance. But he recovered and kept on going.

On the car radio, the announcer said, "It's amazing. After twenty-five miles, that's one hundred laps, folks, the lead rider for the Cutter team is still on his bike without an exchange. His name is Dave Stohler. . . ."

"That's my boy!", Mr. Stohler said proudly. He pushed the gas pedal to the floor, racing the engine, and then grabbed the wheel as if he were in a race himself.

"And he's pulling ahead," the announcer said. He sounded amazed. "He's . . . he's actually pulling ahead. There he goes!"

The thrill of the moment pulled Katherine to her feet. She wanted to yell, but couldn't quite bring herself to do it. She clenched her fists for a moment, tense with excitement, and then sat back down.

Dave was going all out. His left leg was hurting him worse now, he was in terrible pain, but he was still about fifty yards ahead of the closest rider to him. He hoped that was good enough, but if not, there wasn't much he could do about it. He had to get off soon. The pain was too much for him.

As he approached his pit area, he waved to the guys and raised a single finger.

Mike got excited. "We're number one!" he yelled.

Moocher knew better. "No," he said, "he wants off. That's the signal. He's going to go one more lap."

178

"Ooops!" Cyril said.

It took a minute for the meaning of the situation to sink in. Then Mike said, "You mean one of us ..."

"Once again," Cyril said, "I say, oops!"

Mike looked terrified.

Up in the reviewing stand, the President of the university was looking at Dave through a pair of binoculars. Dave, knowing he was on his last lap, was really pouring it on, and he was something to see.

"Well," the President of the university said finally, "I had no idea."

Coming around the final turn, Dave swung off and headed toward the pit area.

In Pit Area No. 34, the guys seemed to be pushing each other forward. None of them wanted to be the one who got on the bike.

Dave roared into this confusion at top speed, slaming on his brakes and jumping off, all in one motion. He took a running step, his left leg collapsed, and then he crumpled to the ground.

Moocher and Cyril helped pull him to his feet. That left Mike standing alone, holding the bike, which he was quick enough to catch just before it fell.

"Go, Mike!" Dave said, grimacing in pain.

Mike was looking at the bike as if he didn't know what it was for.

Moocher got mad. "We've got a lead, idiot," he yelled at Mike. "Get going!"

But there were too many things going on. The crowd, the other riders staring at him, the pressure of the moment, all these things proved too much for Mike. In that moment, he learned something about himself that he did not especially want to know. He was not a clutch player.

He kept staring at the bike, as their lead evaporated like dew on a windshield.

The other riders were catching up, and Moocher couldn't take it any more.

He pushed Mike away, grabbed the bike, and jumped on.

Moocher had great intentions, and short legs. He found out very quickly that if he sat on the seat he couldn't reach the pedals. So he decided to ride standing up. As the other teams came around the turn, he took off in this position.

From his place in his pit area, Rod smiled over at Dave. The smile said: What did it get you?

Moocher, still standing up, was giving it all he had. But his short legs had very little thrust in this position, and other teams started to pull away from him.

"It's Sigma Nu, Phi Kappa Psi, Sigma Alpha Epsilon. . . . the Cutters are fading, but it sure was some try," the radio announcer shouted. "Dave Stohler seems to be hurt. The first aid team has reached him. . . ."

Mr. Stohler wasn't in the car lot any more. He was driving through town as fast as he could, on his way to the stadium.

He passed his house, going sixty. For a second, he slowed down, as if wondering whether to pick up his wife, but then he speeded up again and drove on by.

Rushing through the turnstiles at the stadium, he saw a woman looking at him. It took him a moment to realize that the woman was his wife.

With genuine pride he said, "Ev, he sure tried. Even the announcer said so."

"Too bad he . . ." Mrs. Stohler started to say, but her husband wouldn't hear it.

"Too bad nothing," he said.

In Pit No. 34 Mike watched the lead riders race past. Moocher, lagging badly behind them, limped in for an exchange.

Cyril took the bike from him. He didn't even look at Mike. He knew Mike wasn't going to do anything.

Cyril's legs were so long that when he sat on the bike and started to pedal, his knees nearly hit his chin, but he started pumping away just the same and took off after the pack, which was by now far ahead of him.

Mike sat on the bench, his shoulders slumped.

Moocher, exhausted, stumbled over.

"Where's Dave?" he asked.

Mike pointed out toward the track. Dave was in the center of the field, applying medication from a first aid station.

"It's all over," Mike said softly.

Cyril, bent over the bike like a large, ungainly stork, was giving it the best he had. Coming around on his first lap, he passed Pit Area No. 34.

"Help!" he shouted as loud as he could, which got him a couple of laughs from the stand.

Dave was back in the pit, adhesive tape in his hands, and he was about to start binding up his leg.

Rod rode past, well in the lead. Dave and Mike looked at one another. Each knew what the other was thinking.

When Rod pulled into his pit area, relinquishing his bike to a teammate, the three black riders in Pit Area No. 4 began planning strategy.

"Looks like they're gonna save Rod for the sprint," one of them said. He pointed to a teammate. "You get on when he does. Stay behind him until the last turn. . . ."

Nothing approaching that kind of constructive thinking was going on in Pit Area No. 34. Moocher was exhausted. He lay on his back, completely absorbed with the difficult problem of breathing. Dave sat, staring into space. He was as depressed as he had ever been in his life. He still held adhesive tape in his hand, but could not bring himself to tackle the job of putting it on his leg.

When Cyril came in for an exchange, Mike stood up and grabbed the bike. He hesitated for a moment, and then jumped on. Cyril collapsed on the ground near Dave, an incongruous smile on his face.

"We're doing better than I thought we would," he said gasping for breath.

Now that he was actually on the thing, Mike was giving it everything he had. He was riding like a bull, charging like mad. He gave it more than he needed to, substituting strength for skill, and drifted out in the turns. Coming around a turn, he almost rode into Pit Area No. 1, where Rod was resting. Rod smiled that Texas smile, and Mike wanted to smash the bike right into him, but it was more important to beat him on the track. This near miss got Mike back in the groove, and he started paying attention to what he was doing.

In Pit Area No. 34, Moocher and Cyril sat close together, watching Mike, looking quite satisfied. Dave, feeling a surge of pride, forgot about his leg for a minute.

Out on the infield, Mike's brother, the campus cop, waved his cap excitedly as Mike rode past him.

"C'mon, you cutter!" Mike's brother yelled.

Dave looked out across the field. He noticed two people standing in the infield opposite his pit area, waving at him. He looked closer. The people were his parents. They were obviously proud of him, and were waving to indicate that.

Nancy came into the pit area to congratulate them. Not just Moocher, all of them.

"I've never seen anyone try so hard," she said. "I'm proud of you."

Cyril smiled up at her. "We showed them, huh?"

Dave jumped up. He'd heard that talk all his life, and he was getting tired of it. Dumb cutters, congratulating themselves for having put up a good fight at the same time they were resigning themselves to losing. Just this once, maybe it didn't have to be that way.

"Anybody can try!" he snapped at them, and walked, limping slightly, toward the track.

Mike, who was ready to fall off the bike

183

from exhaustion, looked longingly at the ground below him, thinking it might be wonderful to just fall off in a slow sidewise roll and lie down and sleep for a week. Lifting his heavy head, he saw, to his surprise, that Dave was waving at him to come in. Mike, in his condition, had no idea what was going on and wasn't about to argue. Besides, he told himself, Dave knew more about this stuff than he did.

He brought the bike in too fast, but managed to brake in time to avoid crashing into Nancy and his teammates. He got off the bike, wobbling like a drunk.

Dave got on, shakily. Moocher, realizing what was going on, ran up and held Dave in place, trying to steady him. Then Cyril realized what was about to take place. He took the adhesive tape that Dave had left behind and started wrapping it around Dave's feet, taping them to the pedals.

Between heavy, racking breaths, Mike was collapsed on the bench, managed to ask, "What's going on?"

"It's like Charlton Heston in *El Cid*," Cyril told him, which was as much of an explanation as he was going to get out of Cyril.

"They're going to lap us," Mike said.

The three black riders, still deep in their strategy session, looked up, astonished, to see Dave, whom they'd counted out of the race, go whizzing past them.

Rod saw Dave, too. The rider for his team was not far behind. "C'mon! C'mon!" Rod shouted at his teammate. "You got him!"

Mr. and Mrs. Stohler, who had resigned themselves to loss, were astonished, but delighted, to see Dave back on the bike.

Mrs. Stohler cupped her hands over her mouth to make a megaphone and shouted, as loud as she could, "Go, son, go!"

Back in Pit Area No. 34, the guys were jumping up and down again, and slapping each other on the back.

Dave was coming around the turn. He was gaining, making up for lost ground.

He could see his teammates jumping up and down with excitement. He saw his parents' mouths moving and knew they were shouting encouragement at him, but he couldn't exactly hear them. He couldn't hear the crowd, either, though he knew it was screaming.

That music was back in his head again, the music he always heard when he was riding well, when he was cooking, when he felt the exhilaration he only felt on a bike. Mendelssohn's "Italian Symphony" was with him again. So what if he wasn't Italian. Mendelssohn wasn't Italian, either. The music pulsed through his body giving him energy, carrying him along. And his face showed the emotion of giving himself over to it, and—maybe—of saying goodbye to it, too.

As Dave sped past their pit area, the three black riders exchanged glances, each one evidently hoping that one of the others had an answer. The three of them had the unmistakable look of people who know that their plan is not going to work and that they are going to have to come up with another one.

The college guys in Pit Area No. 1 were watching, too. They were shaking their heads from side to side, trying to convince themselves and each other that Dave couldn't possibly catch up.

At the big board, the operator flipped another lap card: 5 to go.

Rod jumped up from the bench, ready to take the exchange for his final sprint.

The black sprinter got up, too. He and Rod looked over at each other. Then they both looked over to the track to see Dave coming up behind the three lead riders in the race, inexorable and inescapable.

Rod and the black guy mounted their bikes exactly the same instant and started to accelerate.

Then Dave passed the third rider from the lead group, and now there were just Rod and the black guy up ahead of him, and Dave knew they could feel him behind them, gaining.

The lap board now read 1. One last lap to go. An official out on the field waved a flag, signaling this fact to the riders. As Rod and the black guy rode past the man, Dave was right behind them, and getting closer. And pouring it on.

In the backstretch of the last lap, Rod and the black guy were riding abreast. Dave, right behind them, was getting tired of looking at their backs. The Italian music playing in his head told him he didn't have to. The Italian music gave him that little extra push he needed to catch up and pull in behind Rod, who was riding on the inside. They started around the curve. Rod, probably getting tired, drifted out a bit, just a hair toward the outside. and that was all the room and all the break Dave needed.

He shot for the inside edge and took it as they came around the final turn.

All three of them stood up from their seats and began pumping away, knowing this was their final sprint.

As they headed for the finish line, anyone in the stands would have called it dead even.

There were still about forty yards to go, and Dave suddenly exploded ahead like he'd been shot out of a cannon, finding in himself an inner resource that neither of the other two guys possessed. Where it came from he could not have said, but whatever it was, he had it, and it gave him the edge, and he shot out ahead and over the finish line a scant inch or so ahead of the other two riders. He raised his arms in the air like a champion, and it was the purest moment he had ever known.

The guys ran toward him. His best buddies, Cyril, Mike, and Moocher. They were jubilant. They were so jubilant they knocked him down, but Dave didn't mind at all.

Then the others started rushing toward the pit.

Nancy, in her waitress uniform, grabbed Moocher and kissed him, practically lifting him off the ground.

Mike's brother embraced Mike with a feeling of family pride, something that had been missing for far too long.

Dave's parents rushed up to their son, waving and shouting. Mr. Stohler seemed quite out of control, not knowing what to say or do first.

There was a lot of shouting and cheering. Confetti filled the air.

Cyril stood off to the side, watching it

all. He felt happy and excluded at the same time. Everybody was hugging and being hugged, except for him. He thought it was a nice time, anyway. He was glad they had won. He wondered what his father would find to say. Congratulating winners was something his father didn't know much about. Maybe that was why he wasn't there.

Up in the stands, Katherine was watching the scene below. She had gotten up to leave half a dozen times during the afternoon, but she was still in the stands at the end.

She looked over at Dave, now surrounded by admirers and not at all used to it.

Over at Pit No. 1, she could see Rod, keeping a stiff upper lip, trying to smile, to understand why he hadn't won, why money, genes, membership in a fraternity, and the other natural advantages had not guaranteed victory for him.

Katherine missed them both but felt, to her surprise, that she didn't have anything to say to either of them. "Good-bye," she whispered to herself, and she started down the stadium stairs, leaving a part of her life behind her.

Dave left the stadium with his parents. Mike left arm in arm with his brother. Moocher and Nancy walked off, holding hands.

Cyril had all four trophies under his arms. All of the guys had gone in separate directions, and he didn't know which one to follow.

The wind blew the confetti up around his ankles. He didn't notice it, and kept on walking.

188

15

The wind kept on blowing, and it was suddenly fall.

Leaves became golden yellow and fell off the trees, swirling in the air, falling on the road.

Mike's car had to plow through a near tunnel of leaves as it made its way up the entrance ramp to the Thruway.

He had a cigarette in his mouth, unlit. He had a Stetson on, low over his eyes. He was heading out West. The guys weren't going, but he was. He passed a sign saying YOU ARE NOW LEAVING BLOOMINGTON and pointed his car toward the Western skies, the open plains, and all possibilities stretching out before him.

There was a new business in Bloomington:

CUTTER CARS LTD. Cars gleamed in the fall sunlight. QUARRY SPECIAL, a sign on a windshield said.

A very pregnant Mrs. Stohler was sweeping leaves off the lot. Mr. Stohler was preparing to mount a bicycle to take his daily ride exercise.

The leaves were falling on the campus, too, swirling around, blowing in the wind.

Students walked back and forth along the walks, shuffling through the leaves. Dave was pushing a bike along, his own Italian-made bike, whistling as he walked. He was wearing a satin warmup jacket, and on the back of it said PHI KAPPA PSI.

An attractive girl, looking quite lost, walked up to him. When she spoke, it was with an obvious French accent, which Dave found most attractive:

"Par*don*", she said, putting the accent on the last syllable. "Do you know where is the office of the Pursar?"

Dave suddenly lost his new-found college cool in the warmth of the French girl's smile. She reminded him of somebody.

Music began playing in his head. French music. Wonderful cabaret music, with accordions.

"Pursar?" he said. "Oh, you mean the Bursar's office."

"*Oui*," the girl said, in a way to break his heart. "Bursar."

"You're," Dave said hesitating, "you're French, eh?"

She smiled sweetly.

Mr. Stohler was riding around the campus on his bike. He took this route almost every day now. He didn't feel out of place, because after all, his son was a student, and he had helped build the place.

Dave and the French girl were riding double on his bike. In the girls' arms were Dave's school books; the top book was called *Beginning French*.

"French is my major," Dave was telling her over his shoulder. "It's just my first year, of course. Have you ever seen Le Tour de France?" He gave these last words his best French accent.

"No," the girl said.

"No!" he said, in astonishment. How could such a wonderful girl not have seen Le Tour de France? His accent and gestures became more French: "Oh, *mon Dieu*. But the French riders... they are the best. Pouladoir! Anquetil!"

He was in the middle of his speech when his father rode by in the opposite direction.

"Hello, there, big shot," his father called out, waving.

"*Bonjour*, Papa," Dave said.

Mr. Stohler's head swirled in its socket. Uh, oh, he said to himself. He recognized the symptoms. He shrugged his shoulders, smiling to himself, and rode off, wondering if a French son would be an improvement. . . .

Dave, meanwhile, was gearing up to his new fantasy. The girl's hair was blowing wildly in the wind, grazing his cheeks and swirling around his head.

"*Je, m'appelle*. . . ." he began, gesturing with his hand. . . .